As a young man, **Edgar Lee Masters** (1869–1950) rebelled against what he believed to be the hypocrisy of small-town life and went to Chicago, where he practiced law for thirty years. He published eleven books of verse, plays, and essays before beginning his masterpiece, *Spoon River Anthology* (1915). Later, Masters, Carl Sandburg, and Vachel Lindsay initiated a poetic renaissance in the Midwest, with Chicago as its center.

John Hollander (1929–2013) was an acclaimed American poet and the Sterling Professor emeritus of English at Yale University. His books include *Spectral Emanations: New and Selected Poems*, *Harp Lake*, *In Time and Place*, and *Blue Wine and Other Poems*. Hollander was also the author of a number of critical works, including *Rhyme's Reason: A Guide to English Verse*.

Ronald Primeau is Professor of English and Director of the MA in Humanities at Central Michigan University. He has published books on Edgar Lee Masters, Herbert W. Martin, the literature of the American highway, and the rhetoric of television. He has edited works on Masters, Paul Laurence Dunbar, and the dynamics of literary influence.

Spoon River Anthology

EDGAR LEE MASTERS

*With an Introduction by John Hollander
and an Afterword by Ronald Primeau*

SIGNET CLASSICS

SIGNET CLASSICS
Published by the Penguin Group
Penguin Group (USA) LLC, 375 Hudson Street,
New York, New York 10014

USA | Canada | UK | Ireland | Australia | New Zealand | India | South Africa | China
penguin.com
A Penguin Random House Company

Published by Signet Classics, an imprint of New American Library,
a division of Penguin Group (USA) LLC

First Signet Classics Printing, January 1992
First Signet Classics Printing (Primeau Afterword), July 2007

ISBN 978-0-451-53058-5

Printed in the United States of America
30   29   28   27   26   25   24   23

Contents

Introduction

———

Spoon River Anthology is one of those remarkable, seemingly sui generis American books, like William Carlos Williams' *Spring and All*, or John Dos Passos' *U.S.A.*, which seem to mark milestones in the long, strange course of our country's attempts to understand itself. It creates a fictional community through the short dramatic monologues spoken by its deceased inhabitants, rather than by overt description. The town is more like Edwin Arlington Robinson's Tilbury Town (something like Robinson's own home of Gardiner, Maine)—and certainly more like Sherwood Anderson's Winesburg, Ohio—than like Sinclair Lewis' Gopher Prairie (in *Main Street*) or Thornton Wilder's Grover's Corners, New Hampshire (*Our Town*) or, of course, Faulkner's Jefferson in his Yoknapatawpha County. Its author was a Chicago lawyer, a political progressive, a literary figure (in the circle of Theodore Dreiser, Vachel Lindsay, and Carl Sandburg, among others), womanizer, and quite uninspired poet, who in the unique format, and under unique imaginative pressures, excelled himself by producing a masterpiece.

The volume appeared for the first time in 1915 and, in the expanded form in which we now know it (with thirty-five added epitaphs), in the following year, just three-quarters of a century ago. It was an immediate success, praised extravagantly—and alternately condemned—for its skeptical energy, erotic specificity, reforming nay-saying coupled with romantic transcendent yearnings, and unfamiliar structure and mode of verse. It went through seventy editions in many languages, and remained a canonical work which was itself widely and heavily anthologized. Over the years since World War II it seemed to wear less well, possibly because it was most widely known through snippets, separate portraits that appeared in anthologies but which would not allow any of the book's quasi-narrative and schematic structures to emerge. As individual "poems," the individual epitaphs have far less power than they do in context. But a fresh look at the whole volume today—and at a time when the sexual and political issues raised in it are totally tame, and a vernacular vers libre has replaced rhymed jingle as the mode in which "everybody" writes—reveals a splendidly durable, fascinating, and moving book.

An "anthology" is, in its literal Greek sense, a garland or bouquet of flowers, applied originally to a collection of epigrams compiled, on the basis of many earlier ones, in the tenth century A.D. (the so-called *Palatine Anthology*). The term subsequently became used for collections of verse by various authors (although in Elizabethan England they were called "miscellanies") and, significantly, in the title of the massive collection of American poetry, *An American Anthology*, edited by Edmund Clarence Stedman in 1900. But it is the little poems of the so-called *Greek Anthology* which Masters had most directly in mind, and particularly the sepulchral epigrams of Book VII. These are actual or, more usually, fictional epitaphs, sometimes of only one couplet, sometimes of greater length. Among them are the famous words of Simonides, quoted by Herodotus, for the Spartans killed at the battle of Thermopylae (480 B.C.); as they might be put in the standard English epigrammatic meter:

Tell them in Sparta, you who now pass by
That here obedient to their laws we lie.

Verse epitaphs like this one typically speak for the deceased, asking the passerby—in the words of old-fashioned railway crossings—to "stop, look, listen," to contemplate for a moment something of the life of the deceased as the occasion for a general memento mori, a reminder of death. Alternately, it is the monument or grave marker personified that does the speaking. The dead on The Hill in Spoon River speak variously: directly, like Mary McNeely; or to the reader figuratively, as "passer-by"; to the citizens of the town (as if Simonides had written "O Spartans, . . ."); or to one another. Their rhetorical modes are various, and their verbal actions include confession, plea, naive and devious expression, ironic narrative, and wide-reaching parable. In the pairings and sometimes larger sequential groupings of speaking graves, the reader frequently comes upon a narrative constructed by the corrective view of the subsequent speaker. From the totality of these, there emerges the nature of the town itself and the way in which it is made to function as a representation of American life, both rural and urban.

The individual epitaphs were originally published in separate "garlands." The first one appeared in *Reedy's Mirror*, a St. Louis periodical, on May 29, 1914. It consisted of the framing poem "The Hill"—a traditional exercise in the medieval *ubi sunt?* ("where are they now?") formula, best known in the later nineteenth century through Dante Gabriel Rossetti's translation of François Villon's ballade with the refrain "And where are the snows of yester-year?" Following it, and under slightly different names, were the epitaphs of Hod Putt (with its resonantly biting repetition of the phrase "the bankrupt law" to mean not the federal Bankruptcy Act of 1898, but

rather the institution of the Law itself, having exhausted all its store of Justice), Ollie McGee, The Unknown, Cassius Hueffer, Serepta Mason, Amanda
Barker, and Chase Henry, for example. Even in this
small group, we can note the emergence of a pattern
which would recur throughout the completed book:
The portraits of Serepta Mason and Amanda Barker
form a kind of loosely related diptych (and, with the
addition of Constance Hately in the 1916 edition, a
grim triptych).

The way in which the reader gathers information
about individual people, families, and the economic,
political, and social structure of the town, learns the
other side of an apparently authoritatively stated
story, or discovers that a seemingly finished matter
was really a loose end, forms the basic fabric of the
book. The opening diptych of Ollie and Fletcher
McGee enacts a radical revision and warns us that
our responses to and feelings about the personages
talking from beyond the grave must school themselves in ironic wisdom. The four panels of the Pantier family and Emily Sparks also look ahead to the
stories of Dora Williams and her mother, which in
turn will engage those of Roscoe and Mrs. Purkapile.
(The Pantier family's tale will be further glossed by
the complaining question of the zealous and puritani-
cal A. D. Blood, himself revealed as a murderer later
on, "Why do you let the milliner's daughter Dora,/
And the worthless son of Benjamin Pantier/Nightly
make my grave their unholy pillow?") The five-
paneled group starting with Washington McNeely's
epitaph is another such, as is the three-epitaph group
starting with Tom Merritt's in which violence unfolds
subsequently into judicial and moral horrors. The poetess Minerva Jones is raped by "Butch" Weldy,
whose monologue ends a five-part sequence but is
reengaged in the later story of Roy Butler. Weldy,
long after having been blinded in an accident, serves

as foreman of the jury falsely convicting Butler of a
rape he never committed. This is the most frequent
pattern of narrative connection, often involving the
much-delayed discovery of an interlocking of lives.

Sometimes the diptychs frame an ironic contrast,
such as those of the amoral newspaperman, Editor
Whedon, and his devout progressive neighbor on
The Hill and in these pages, Carl Hamblin (his epitaph contains a fierce excoriation of badly institu-
tionalized Justice, and involves a brilliant rereading
of her traditional emblematic blindness and sword).
Sometimes a sequence of several pairings develops
an emphatic momentary narrative rhythm. Thus we
have the paired graves of Elsa Wertman and the
unknowing, and therefore tragically ironic, boast of
Hamilton Greene; followed by the paired philosophical meditation and violently unphilosophical
stories of Ernest Hyde and Roger Heston; followed
in turn by the Sibleys, the eternally cuckolded
preacher and his gnomic, chthonic, *Ewigweiblichen*
wife, whose secret lies (quite shockingly for 1915,
one would guess) "Under a mound that you shall
never find"—a mons veneris itself under a burial
mound. And there are the paralleled but unpaired
musicians, Fiddler Jones—that avatar of the grass-
hopper or cicada of the well-known Greek Anacre-
ontic poem—and Blind Jack, with his higher,
Homeric vision. But there are other less formal pat-
ternings that arise as well: the different modes of
parable propounded by Samuel Gardner and Dow
Kritt, Browningesque and Blakeian, respectively (and
William Goode's seems almost a parable Robert Frost
might have played with, but not so baldly). For un-
derlying all of the patterns of relation among the individual portraits is the tangle of lines of power
emanating from the banker Rhodes and his judicial,
clerical, and journalistic deputies. It is this structure,
together with the relations outlined above—some the-

matic, some narrative, some rhetorical—that hold the book, and the fiction of the town, together.

An exemplary and powerful instance of the way in which one story will undercut another is that of Knowlt Hoheimer's little story:

I was the first fruits of the battle of Missionary Ridge.
When I felt the bullet enter my heart
I wished I had staid at home and gone to jail
For stealing the hogs of Curl Trenary,
Instead of running away and joining the army.
Rather a thousand times the county jail
Than to lie under this marble figure with wings,
And this granite pedestal
Bearing the words, *"Pro Patria."*
What do they mean, anyway?

The mild irony of the sadly familiar and frequent occasion for military enlistment is underlined sharply by the superb ending: Poor Knowlt doesn't know what the Latin words "mean" because he doesn't know any Latin, much less the rest of the famous tag from Horace, *dulce et decorum est pro patria mori*— Wilfred Owen, in a great poem about World War I, called it "the old lie"—expressing the dubious sentiment that it's lovely and appropriate to die for your country. But he asks the question for Masters' intended sophisticated reader, who knows all that, but who must be made to ask a higher, moral question: What can *"patria"* mean if it kills its sons? All this is very effective. But then the story is glossed— although hardly authoritatively—by Lydia Puckett, the next speaker:

Knowlt Hoheimer ran away to the war
The day before Curl Trenary
Swore out a warrant through Justice Arnett
For stealing hogs.
But that's not the reason he turned a soldier.

> He caught me running with Lucius Atherton.
> We quarreled and I told him never again
> To cross my path.
> Then he stole the hogs and went to the war—
> Back of every soldier is a woman.

Well, she would say that. And the real story remains
midway between their versions of it, even as it embraces both his ironic question and her home truth.

There are even subtler juxtapositions, of a purely
poetic rather than a narrative sort, as well. For example, the epitaph of the boy called simply "The Unknown" (pointedly not an Unknown Soldier—its
Ancient Marineresque killing of a hawk strangely an-
ticipates a major poem of Robert Penn Warren's)
ends with the dead boy recounting how

> Daily I search the realms of Hades
> For the soul of the hawk,
> That I may offer him the friendship
> Of one whom life wounded and caged.

His short story is juxtaposed with the shortest of all
the epitaphs, that of Alexander Throckmorton, who
is hardly a presence at all, but a mere voice for framing one of the oldest of paradoxes:

> In youth my wings were strong and tireless,
> But I did not know the mountains.
> In age I knew the mountains
> But my weary wings would not follow my vision—
> Genius is wisdom and youth.

Far more poignant than the contrast between two
very different senses of lost youth here is the way in
which the trope of the hawk, used parabolically by
Throckmorton, seems to have flown in from the preceding poem. Such nuances as these are seemingly

far from the agenda of the book's sardonic iconoclasm.

Among the citizens are all manner of men and women, practitioners of many trades and crafts, village atheists, philosophers and layabouts, many lawyers and several writers, including sad bad poets like Petit and comically bad ones like Jonathan Swift Somers (his broadly Miltonic parody, *The Spooniad*, appears at the end of the volume, just before the unfortunate "Epilogue" added in 1916, with its rhymed verse and weak echoes of Goethe and Shelley). Many of them are persons of the sort Sherwood Anderson would shortly afterward call "grotesques." There are several suicides, and a good many victims of murder, fraud, injustice, religious subjection, and spiritual death, and the procession of malefactors, victims, and wretches throughout the first half of the book is indeed a dismal one.

This view from the dark side of The Hill, as it were, suggests that the *communitas* of the town of Spoon River is maintained in two modes, Public and Private. In the Public realm Courthouse (and understandably, there are a good many lawyers in Spoon River), Church, Press, and Pulpit are the institutional instruments, with Thomas Rhodes' Bank remaining always the center of power and control, even as the epitaph of the man himself occurs at the center of the book (in the 1915 edition, it was the 104th out of 210). Most of those in power are seen as morally corrupt, although in each sphere there are antithetical figures, usually lonely in some way. The Private realm is that of the horrors, despairs, and human abuses of sexual and family life, and it is the internalized "institutions"—of erotic repression, guilt, fear, and quiet and unquiet desperation, among others—which seem to move among these lives from the inside in response to the forces exerted by Money and Law from without.

But the moral map of the town is not only drawn
on the projection of the turn-of-the-century muckrak-
ing reformer, with many of whose views Masters was
indeed sympathetic (but indeed, with a mature skepticism of some of the simple pieties of populism, as in
John Hancock Otis' view of Anthony Findlay, whose
monologue follows his). He puts the epitaphs of "the
fools, the drunkards, and the failures" first; it is from
their stories that we infer the character and opera-
tions of the villains. Toward the end of the anthology
come the monologues of "the heroes and the enlightened spirits," although these seem inevitably less
forceful than the earlier ones. (In between—in what
he admitted was a Dantean progression—Masters
placed the souls of what he called "people of one-
birth minds.") Among the "enlightened spirits" are
the amateur scientists; the astronomer; the village
atheist; Father Malloy—the one cleric exempt from
the charge of corruption: in the almost totally Protes-
tant town he is an exotic and spiritually rich outsider,
and counts for Masters as a secular flame and rock;
the skeptic Scholfield Huxley and the prophets Isaiah
Beethoven and Elijah Browning (and all these mani-
fest the allusive naming, sometimes heavily ironic,
in the latter part of the book, e.g., Voltaire Johnson,
Hamlet Micure).

The collection concludes with the Apollonian invocation of Webster Ford (the name Masters frequently used as a nom de plume, and particularly
for the authorship of the separate "garlands" of epitaphs he originally published), and is thereby to be
considered his own notional epitaph. In addition,
there is that of Percival Sharp. The distinguished
poet May Swenson felt that this epitaph was also
Masters' own; it certainly appears to be so in a
stronger, perhaps less literal, way. And it certainly
embodies the renaissance *topos* of poetic perpetua-
tion, best known from Shakespeare's sonnet "Not

marble, nor the gilded monuments/Of princes shall outlive this powerful rhyme." It concludes ". . . for myself I know/I stirred certain vibrations in Spoon River/Which are my true epitaph, more lasting than stone" which rings with the irony of this fictive inscription on the fictive tombstone of an imaginary person; it is indeed the "true epitaph" of Masters the poet, "more lasting" than any literal stone, or than all the rest of his minor, though ambitious verse.

Masters had published two minor volumes of poems, in 1898 and 1910, before his one major book. Subsequent to it, he brought out thirteen more, including *The New Spoon River*. A sequel published in 1924, *The New Spoon River* contains 318 new epitaphs, some of considerable interest, but many with less force and either individuation or interconnectedness than marked the original book. After the immediate success of the first *Spoon River Anthology*, Masters moved to New York, where he continued to live and write thereafter, giving up his law practice in 1920 and subsequently publishing five novels, plays, several biographies, a memoir, and a history of the Sangamon River before his death in 1950.

He was born in Garnett, Kansas, in 1869, but his family soon moved to Illinois, and he grew up in the region around Springfield. After a year at Knox College in Galesburg, Illinois (at which time he studied Greek and became acquainted with some of the classics), he returned to study law privately. In 1892 he moved to Chicago, gradually building up a good law practice, and becoming more and more involved with the literary life of the city. It was in Chicago that he began writing and eventually publishing, while still enjoying the intellectual challenge and the sociological insights gained from a legal practice sometimes made difficult for him by his radical views. "The law had been an X ray to me, and many kinds of chemicals," he wrote later of the relation between his legal work and his imaginative literature.

While J. W. Mackail's elegant prose translations of *Select Epigrams from the Greek Anthology* (revised edition, 1906)—which Masters had perhaps seen earlier but which his friend and editor William Marion Reedy had apparently given him in 1913—may have been an enabling force for him, so perhaps was a visit from his mother to Chicago in May of 1914 a precipitating one. They talked much of "the whole past Lewistown and Petersburg," bringing up people and events he had forgotten and tracing "those persons to their final fates." Some days later, just after her departure, he started on "The Hill" and a few of the first portraits in what would be the anthology. But he was also conflating these impulses with another, long-abandoned one. A decade earlier, he had thought of a novel that might represent and embody an entire town. In his memoir, *Across Spoon River* (1936), he recalls asking, "Why not make this book the book I had thought about in 1906, in which I should draw the macrocosm by portraying the microcosm? Why not put side by side the stories of two characters interlocked by fate, thus giving both misunderstood souls a chance to be justly weighed?" But that very same earlier unwritten book had perhaps its own earlier source.

In 1903, Masters had entered into a law partnership, which lasted eight years, with the subsequently illustrious Clarence Darrow. Darrow himself published in 1904 a book called *Farmington*, a strangely lyrical novel done as a set of sketches about a small Pennsylvania town. It probably influenced Masters strongly, at first in his desire to write that novel about a town in Illinois, and eventually in the transmutation of that intention in Spoon River. Darrow's chapter on the town's burying ground, creeping in time up a hill from the churchyard, may have been particularly resonant, as in a moment like this:

> I think the first time my faith was shaken in any-
> thing I saw on a gravestone was when I chanced
> upon a brand-new slab erected to the memory of
> the town drunkard by his "loving wife and chil-
> dren." The inscription said that the deceased was
> a kind and loving husband and a most indulgent
> father. Everyone in Farmington knew that the wife
> had often called in the constable to protect her
> from the husband; but still here was the stone. Yet,
> after all, the inscription may not have been untrue;
> indeed, it may have been more truthful than those
> that rested above many a man and woman who
> had lived and died without reproach. (p. 126)

This is the sort of conjecture which lies behind the
epitaph of Chase Henry (one of the first published),
Spoon River's town drunkard, and the wry observa-
tion of Judge Somers that he, the erudite lawyer, lies
"unmarked, forgotten,/While Chase Henry, the town
drunkard,/Has a marble block, topped by an urn,/
Wherein Nature, in a mood ironical, [and here, the
high, inverted diction itself produces an ironic tone]/
Has sown a flowering weed?" Generally, it raises the
question of undecidable narrations, one which Browning's great *The Ring and the Book* raised for Masters
with lasting effect, for it gives local narrative force
to the diptychs and polyptychs and deferred pairings
of epitaphs, one correcting, revising, making ironic
in retrospect the special pleading of an earlier one,
basically supplying the "plot" of the whole sequence,
aside from what the author acknowledged to be the
nineteen stories "developed by interrelated portraits."

Literary allusion and echo aside, historical allusive-
ness is everywhere present in the book, with a range
of degrees and modes of irony, in the names of the
dead citizens of Spoon River. Masters reported later
that he had drawn most of the names "from both the
Spoon River and Sangamon River cemeteries, com-

bining first names here with surnames there . . ." but
the names on The Hill represent a broad spectrum
of modes of fictional naming. There are the sorts of
names from eighteenth-century drama and fiction,
like those of Penniwit the Artist or Petit the (obviously minor and trivial) Poet (opposed to Theodore
the Poet, more a self-portrait of Masters himself).
There is the Dickensian-Dostoeyvskian sort of fantastic name which evokes, less literally but through near
puns, something of character: It has been remarked
that "Hod Putt," the opening portrait of the anthology, with his grim observations on bankruptcy, is
indeed "hard put." There are the allusive associa-
tions of names like that of the town banker (evoking
that of Cecil Rhodes, colonial entrepreneur of Africa),
and the pointed irony of that of Robert Southey
Burke, for example, alluding to the English romantic
poet scorned by Byron and others for selling out to
arch conservatism. Or there is the broad irony in the
name of Georgine Sand Miner, the shallow, vengeful
and unproductive echo of the free-living and high-
minded pseudonymous French novelist. Or in that
of W. Lloyd Garrison Standard, no moral kin of the
great abolitionist.

   The fictional community of Spoon River itself reflects the actual name of the river in central Illinois,
and the towns of Lewisburg situated on it and Petersburg on the Sangamon, from the latter to the former
of which Masters' family had moved in his youth.
There are in fact seven actual historical personages
buried on The Hill, although two of them—Davis and
Lucinda Matlock—are given a changed surname; they
are Squire Davis and his wife, Lucinda [Wasson] Masters, the poet's paternal grandparents. John and Rebecca Wasson were indeed his great-great-grandparents.
The other three figures are all constellated around
Lincoln: his law partner and biographer, Herndon,
his supposed early love, Ann Rutledge, and, most

interestingly, a woman named Hannah Armstrong, whose story slightly fictionalizes the historical facts on which it is based.

When Abraham Lincoln lived in Salem, Illinois, from 1830 to 1836, he knew Jack Armstrong and his wife, Hannah. In 1857, their son William Duff Armstrong was indicted for murder in connection with a tavern brawl; on the basis of old friendship, Hannah wrote to Lincoln, by then a successful lawyer and at an important point in his political career, asking him to defend her son. He did so, winning the case, in the so-called "almanac trial" (by producing an almanac in court to discredit key prosecution testimony about the height of the moon at the time of the murder, and by convincing the jury that the death had occurred in a drunken fall from a horse). Five years later, with all four of Hannah Armstrong's sons in the army (one, indeed, killed in action and one wounded), and she herself too reticent to write Lincoln in the White House, a common friend communicated with Lincoln to ask him to secure William Duff Armstrong's compassionate discharge; on September 18th of that year, the president sent Hannah Armstrong a telegram announcing that he had granted the request.

This is, of course, not quite the story that Spoon River's Hannah Armstrong tells: There was no "Doug," the letter of petition did not fail, there was no imploring trip to Washington, etc. Masters himself seems to have misremembered parts of it, despite his own friendship, between 1913 and 1925, with John Armstrong, William Duff's son; in his memoir, *Across Spoon River*, he identifies him as "the son of Jack [*sic!*], who had been defended by Lincoln for murder." In recasting the story, though, Masters is not merely misremembering, but pointedly shaping an anecdote to its teller's sentiments. And despite Masters' iconoclastic attitude toward the traditional Lincoln hagiography in his unreliable and biased *Lincoln the Man* (1931), it helps place Lincoln at the book's historical center, like the poet himself, "Talking the while of the early days/And telling stories."

Prior to the *Spoon River Anthology*, Masters had written very conventional verse of a not particularly distinguished sort; and while Goethe, Emerson, Shelley, Browning, and Whitman were all extremely important for him, he had been unable to use his great precursors in the way that strong poets do (as Shelley had stood behind Browning, and both of those behind Thomas Hardy, for example). The interrelated monologues of Browning's *The Ring and the Book* were obviously influential for Masters, and indeed, he imitated aspects of it more obviously in his later work. In *Spoon River Anthology* we find frequent Browningesque rhetorical turns—Joseph Dixon, for example, is an incarnation of Abt Vogler, and his epitaph derives from Browning's music poems generally; the way the parables are strung out at the end of the Davis Matlock and Samuel Gardner poems, and so on.

But as has been noted, J. W. Mackail's prose translations from the *Greek Anthology* seem to have had the precipitating formal effect on his writing, unrelated to matters of deeper influence. (Masters was extremely sophisticated in his knowledge of antecedent free verse in English—in talking of his friend Carl Sandburg, he correctly invokes the Matthew Arnold of "The Strayed Reveller"—a poem which many modernist metrical cranks ignore—Ossian, William Ernest Henley, and the German romantics, as well as Whitman.) He later described the metrical convention of the Spoon River epitaphs as "a kind of free verse which was free as iambic pentameter is free, where the lack of rhyme and the changing caesuras, and the varying meter give scope for emotion and music." In fact, a good deal of the "free verse" in this book is unrhymed accentual-syllabic verse, sometimes only occasionally varied by a shorter line. Obvious cases include Paul McNeely's invocation to his beloved nurse, Jane, which is all in tetrameters, or the accentual four-beat lines of "Bert Kessler," or of the Cavalier historian Jefferson Howard, or the anapest-laden pentameters of Wallace Ferguson's Shelleyan meditation on Geneva. Or "Fletcher McGee" which is almost pure blank ballad stanza throughout (save for the first two stanzas in the conventional alternative 3343, the rest are all quite normal). Or Mrs. Williams, the milliner, Autolycus-like, singing of her wares in emphatic dimeter. Or the hypocrite Elmer Karr grinding out his last six lines in pompous blank verse. Or the classical, often dactyllic pentameters of Thomas Trevelyan's Ovidian reminiscence. The rhythmic variations which keep sounding through these epitaphs give voice to them in a way that much subsequent free verse could not. And in any case, Masters thought of the formal mode of his book as extending, rather than shallowly and (like some American poets of the next fifteen years) modernistically affronting poetic continuity. It is perhaps just that he was able to put his Browningesque impulses to best work in the collected dramatic monologues of these inscriptions, and to write with greater rhythmic interest and power than when he had kept too literally to older modes of variation to "give scope for emotion and music."

In other ways, too, the poetic language of the anthology is far less simple, colloquial, and "modern" than has been observed. When poetic inversions occur, they are often sophisticatedly enlisted in aid of a pointed effect. Lucinda Matlock's "Rambled over the fields where sang the larks" should by all rights be "where the larks sang"; but the immediate context is an allusion to an Edenic context, and the lines establishing it are pure Milton:

> I made the garden, and for holiday
> Rambled over the fields where sang the larks,
> And by Spoon River gathering many a shell,
> And many a flower and medicinal weed

Or, again, the Miltonic mode—this time, of enjambment—in the first two lines of the epitaph of the prostitute Rosie Roberts: "I was sick, but more than that, I was mad/At the crooked police, and the crooked game of life," with its discovered revision *"mad at"* = *angry* for *"mad"* = *insane*. There are also many echoic fragments appearing here and there; thus, at the end of "Sexsmith the Dentist" (whose profession is established, it seems, merely to give him the terms for a final metaphor) we get two lines suggesting a Kipling ballad (read these as if the line preceding them ended in "old"): "Why, a moral truth is a hollow tooth/ Which must be propped with gold." Webster Ford's own meters, by the way, from the second through the twenty-third lines of his piece, are all powerfully rhythmic accentual five-beat lines—pentameters with added anapests—but at the very end we get an unrhymed Sapphic stanza invoking the whole preceding book's "leaves of me":

> Too sere for coronal wreaths, and fit alone
> For urns of memory, treasured, perhaps, as themes
> For hearts heroic, fearless singers and livers—
> Delphic Apollo!

Webster Ford's epitaph, as was previously observed, concludes the collection, and functions as a kind of *envoi* for Masters' own work. In modern America, the pure heroic has become impossible, but there was a modernist time during which the conjunction of rage at evil and injustice and overleaping hopefulness constituted a sort of democratic nobility of the spirit. *Spoon River Anthology* partakes of this.

And in addition, it has by now become so much part of the American literary landscape that nature has begun to imitate it: I recall a friend's telling me—to my initial disbelief—of a brief epitaph on a tombstone in a Key West cemetery: *"I told you I was sick."* It sounded like a line by a Borscht Circuit stand-up comic, but the inscription, I have since been assured, is indeed there. And all one needs to do is to imagine for oneself a continuation of its story for two dozen lines or so. It stops being unwittingly funny, and reveals its true origin, on The Hill, in Spoon River.

—John Hollander

Spoon River Anthology

Contents

3

6   *Contents*

Contents

Contents 9

THE HILL

Where are Elmer, Herman, Bert, Tom and Charley,
The weak of will, the strong of arm, the clown, the
    boozer, the fighter?
All, all, are sleeping on the hill.

One passed in a fever,
One was burned in a mine,
One was killed in a brawl,
One died in a jail,
One fell from a bridge toiling for children and wife—
All, all are sleeping, sleeping, sleeping on the hill.

Where are Ella, Kate, Mag, Lizzie and Edith,
The tender heart, the simple soul, the loud, the proud,
    the happy one?—
All, all, are sleeping on the hill.

One died in shameful child-birth,
One of a thwarted love,
One at the hands of a brute in a brothel,
One of a broken pride, in the search for heart's
    desire,
One after life in far-away London and Paris
Was brought to her little space by Ella and Kate and
    Mag—
All, all are sleeping, sleeping, sleeping on the hill.

Where are Uncle Isaac and Aunt Emily,
And old Towny Kincaid and Sevigne Houghton,
And Major Walker who had talked
With venerable men of the revolution?—
All, all, are sleeping on the hill.

*   *   *

They brought them dead sons from the war,
And daughters whom life had crushed,
And their children fatherless, crying—
All, all are sleeping, sleeping, sleeping on the hill.

Where is Old Fiddler Jones
Who played with life all his ninety years,
Braving the sleet with bared breast,
Drinking, rioting, thinking neither of wife nor kin,
Nor gold, nor love, nor heaven?
Lo! he babbles of the fish-frys of long ago,
Of the horse-races of long ago at Clary's Grove,
Of what Abe Lincoln said
One time at Springfield.

HOD PUTT

Here I lie close to the grave
Of Old Bill Piersol,
Who grew rich trading with the Indians, and who
Afterwards took the bankrupt law
And emerged from it richer than ever.
Myself grown tired of toil and poverty
And beholding how Old Bill and others grew in
    wealth,
Robbed a traveler one night near Proctor's Grove,
Killing him unwittingly while doing so,
For the which I was tried and hanged.
That was my way of going into bankruptcy.
Now we who took the bankrupt law in our respec-
    tive ways
Sleep peacefully side by side.

OLLIE McGEE

Have you seen walking through the village
A man with downcast eyes and haggard face?
That is my husband who, by secret cruelty
Never to be told, robbed me of my youth and
    my beauty;
Till at last, wrinkled and with yellow teeth,
And with broken pride and shameful humility,
I sank into the grave.
But what think you gnaws at my husband's heart?
The face of what I was, the face of what he
    made me!
These are driving him to the place where I lie.
In death, therefore, I am avenged.

FLETCHER McGEE

She took my strength by minutes,
She took my life by hours,
She drained me like a fevered moon
That saps the spinning world.
The days went by like shadows,
The minutes wheeled like stars.
She took the pity from my heart,
And made it into smiles.
She was a hunk of sculptor's clay,
My secret thoughts were fingers:
They flew behind her pensive brow
And lined it deep with pain.
They set the lips, and sagged the cheeks,
And drooped the eyes with sorrow.
My soul had entered in the clay,
Fighting like seven devils.
It was not mine, it was not hers;
She held it, but its struggles
Modeled a face she hated,
And a face I feared to see.
I beat the windows, shook the bolts.
I hid me in a corner—
And then she died and haunted me,
And hunted me for life.

ROBERT FULTON TANNER

If a man could bite the giant hand
That catches and destroys him,
As I was bitten by a rat
While demonstrating my patent trap,
In my hardware store that day.
But a man can never avenge himself
On the monstrous ogre Life.
You enter the room—that's being born;
And then you must live—work out your soul,
Aha! the bait that you crave is in view:
A woman with money you want to marry,
Prestige, place, or power in the world.
But there's work to do and things to conquer—
Oh, yes! the wires that screen the bait.
At last you get in—but you hear a step:
The ogre, Life, comes into the room,
(He was waiting and heard the clang of the spring)
To watch you nibble the wondrous cheese,
And stare with his burning eyes at you,
And scowl and laugh, and mock and curse you,
Running up and down in the trap,
Until your misery bores him.

CASSIUS HUEFFER

They have chiseled on my stone the words:
"His life was gentle, and the elements so mixed
    in him
That nature might stand up and say to all the
    world,
This was a man."*
Those who knew me smile
As they read this empty rhetoric.

My epitaph should have been:
"Life was not gentle to him,
And the elements so mixed in him
That he made warfare on life,
In the which he was slain."
While I lived I could not cope with slanderous
    tongues,
Now that I am dead I must submit to an epitaph
Graven by a fool!

*"His life . . . a man." Shakespeare, *Julius Caesar*, V, 5. Marc An-
tony says this of the dead Brutus.

SEREPTA MASON

My life's blossom might have bloomed on all sides
Save for a bitter wind which stunted my petals
On the side of me which you in the village
    could see.
From the dust I lift a voice of protest:
My flowering side you never saw!
Ye living ones, ye are fools indeed
Who do not know the ways of the wind
And the unseen forces
That govern the processes of life.

AMANDA BARKER

Henry got me with child,
Knowing that I could not bring forth life
Without losing my own.
In my youth therefore I entered the portals of dust.
Traveler, it is believed in the village where I lived
That Henry loved me with a husband's love,
But I proclaim from the dust
That he slew me to gratify his hatred.

CONSTANCE HATELY

You praise my self-sacrifice, Spoon River,
In rearing Irene and Mary,
Orphans of my older sister!
And you censure Irene and Mary
For their contempt for me!
But praise not my self-sacrifice,
And censure not their contempt;
I reared them, I cared for them, true enough!—
But I poisoned my benefactions
With constant reminders of their dependence.

CHASE HENRY

In life I was the town drunkard;
When I died the priest denied me burial
In holy ground.
The which redounded to my good fortune.
For the Protestants bought this lot,
And buried my body here,
Close to the grave of the banker Nicholas,
And of his wife Priscilla.
Take note, ye prudent and pious souls,
Of the cross-currents in life
Which bring honor to the dead, who lived in
    shame.

HARRY CAREY GOODHUE

You never marveled, dullards of Spoon River,
When Chase Henry voted against the saloons
To revenge himself for being shut off.
But none of you was keen enough
To follow my steps, or trace me home
As Chase's spiritual brother.
Do you remember when I fought
The bank and the courthouse ring,
For pocketing the interest on public funds?
And when I fought our leading citizens
For making the poor the pack-horses of the taxes?
And when I fought the water works
For stealing streets and raising rates?
And when I fought the business men
Who fought me in these fights?
Then do you remember:
That staggering up from the wreck of defeat,
And the wreck of a ruined career,
I slipped from my cloak my last ideal,
Hidden from all eyes until then,
Like the cherished jawbone of an ass,*
And smote the bank and the water works,
And the business men with prohibition,
And made Spoon River pay the cost
Of the fights that I had lost?

*jawbone of an ass with which Samson smote the Philistines,
Judges 15:15–16

JUDGE SOMERS

How does it happen, tell me,
That I who was most erudite of lawyers,
Who knew Blackstone* and Coke†
Almost by heart, who made the greatest speech
The court-house ever heard, and wrote
A brief that won the praise of Justice Breese—‡
How does it happen, tell me,
That I lie here unmarked, forgotten,
While Chase Henry, the town drunkard,
Has a marble block, topped by an urn,
Wherein Nature, in a mood ironical,
Has sown a flowering weed?

*Blackstone Sir William Blackstone (1723–1780), judge, teacher and
author of the proverbially famous *Commentaries on the Laws of
England*
†Coke Sir Edward Coke (1552–1634), important jurist and parlia-
mentarian
‡Justice Breese Sidney Breese (1800–1878), influential justice of the
Illinois Supreme Court

KINSEY KEENE

Your attention, Thomas Rhodes, president of the
    bank;
Coolbaugh Whedon, editor of the Argus;
Rev. Peet, pastor of the leading church;
A. D. Blood, several times Mayor of Spoon River;
And finally all of you, members of the Social Pu-
    rity Club—
Your attention to Cambronne's dying words,
Standing with the heroic remnant
Of Napoleon's guard on Mount Saint Jean
At the battle field of Waterloo,
When Maitland, the Englishman, called to them:
"Surrender, brave Frenchmen!"—
There at close of day with the battle hopelessly
    lost,
And hordes of men no longer the army
Of the great Napoleon
Streamed from the field like ragged strips
Of thunder clouds in the storm.
Well, what Cambronne said to Maitland
Ere the English fire made smooth the brow of
    the hill
Against the sinking light of day
Say I to you, and all of you,
And to you, O world.
And I charge you to carve it
Upon my stone.

BENJAMIN PANTIER

Together in this grave lie Benjamin Pantier, attor-
    ney at law,
And Nig, his dog, constant companion, solace
    and friend.
Down the gray road, friends, children, men and
    women,
Passing one by one out of life, left me till I was
    alone
With Nig for partner, bed-fellow, comrade in
    drink.
In the morning of life I knew aspiration and saw
    glory.
Then she, who survives me, snared my soul
With a snare which bled me to death,
Till I, once strong of will, lay broken, indifferent,
Living with Nig in a room back of a dingy office.
Under my jaw-bone is snuggled the bony nose of
    Nig—
Our story is lost in silence. Go by, mad world!

MRS. BENJAMIN PANTIER

I know that he told that I snared his soul
With a snare which bled him to death.
And all the men loved him,
And most of the women pitied him.
But suppose you are really a lady, and have deli-
      cate tastes,
And loathe the smell of whiskey and onions.
And the rhythm of Wordsworth's "Ode"* runs in
      your ears,
While he goes about from morning till night
Repeating bits of that common thing;
"Oh, why should the spirit of mortal be proud?"†
And then, suppose:
You are a woman well endowed,
And the only man with whom the law and
      morality
Permit you to have the marital relation
Is the very man that fills you with disgust
Every time you think of it—while you think of it
Every time you see him?
That's why I drove him away from home
To live with his dog in a dingy room
Back of his office.

*Wordsworth's "Ode" the great "Ode: On Intimations of Immor-
tality from Recollections in Early Childhood"
†"Oh, why . . . proud?" William Knox (1789–1825), "Mortality,"
stanza 1.

REUBEN PANTIER

Well, Emily Sparks, your prayers were not wasted
Your love was not all in vain.
I owe whatever I was in life
To your hope that would not give me up,
To your love that saw me still as good.
Dear Emily Sparks, let me tell you the story.
I pass the effect of my father and mother;
The milliner's daughter made me trouble
And out I went in the world,
Where I passed through every peril known
Of wine and women and joy of life.
One night, in a room in the Rue de Rivoli,
I was drinking wine with a black-eyed cocotte,
And the tears swam into my eyes.
She thought they were amorous tears and smiled
For thought of her conquest over me.
But my soul was three thousand miles away,
In the days when you taught me in Spoon River.
And just because you no more could love me,
Nor pray for me, nor write me letters,
The eternal silence of you spoke instead.
And the black-eyed cocotte took the tears for hers,
As well as the deceiving kisses I gave her.
Somehow, from that hour, I had a new vision—
Dear Emily Sparks!

EMILY SPARKS

Where is my boy, my boy—
In what far part of the world?
The boy I loved best of all in the school?—
I, the teacher, the old maid, the virgin heart,
Who made them all my children.
Did I know my boy aright,
Thinking of him as spirit aflame,
Active, ever aspiring?
Oh, boy, boy, for whom I prayed and prayed
In many a watchful hour at night,
Do you remember the letter I wrote you
Of the beautiful love of Christ?
And whether you ever took it or not,
My boy, wherever you are,
Work for your soul's sake,
That all the clay of you, all of the dross of you,
May yield to the fire of you,
Till the fire is nothing but light! . . .
Nothing but light!

TRAINOR THE DRUGGIST

Only the chemist can tell, and not always the
    chemist,
What will result from compounding
Fluids or solids.
And who can tell
How men and women will interact
On each other, or what children will result?
There were Benjamin Pantier and his wife,
Good in themselves, but evil toward each other:
He oxygen, she hydrogen,
Their son, a devastating fire.
I Trainor, the druggist, a mixer of chemicals,
Killed while making an experiment,
Lived unwedded.

DAISY FRASER

Did you ever hear of Editor Whedon
Giving to the public treasury any of the money
    he received
For supporting candidates for office?
Or for writing up the canning factory
To get people to invest?
Or for suppressing the facts about the bank,
When it was rotten and ready to break?
Did you ever hear of the Circuit Judge
Helping anyone except the "Q" railroad,
Or the bankers? Or did Rev. Peet or Rev. Sibley
Give any part of their salary, earned by keeping
    still,
Or speaking out as the leaders wished them to do,
To the building of the water works?
But I—Daisy Fraser who always passed
Along the streets through rows of nods and smiles,
And coughs and words such as "there she goes,"
Never was taken before Justice Arnett
Without contributing ten dollars and costs
To the school fund of Spoon River!

BENJAMIN FRASER

Their spirits beat upon mine
Like the wings of a thousand butterflies.
I closed my eyes and felt their spirits vibrating.
I closed my eyes, yet I knew when their lashes
Fringed their cheeks from downcast eyes,
And when they turned their heads;
And when their garments clung to them,
Or fell from them, in exquisite draperies.
Their spirits watched my ecstasy
With wide looks of starry unconcern.
Their spirits looked upon my torture;
They drank it as it were the water of life;
With reddened cheeks, brightened eyes
The rising flame of my soul made their spirits gilt,
Like the wings of a butterfly drifting suddenly
    into sunlight.
And they cried to me for life, life, life.
But in taking life for myself,
In seizing and crushing their souls,
As a child crushes grapes and drinks
From its palms the purple juice,
I came to this wingless void,
Where neither red, nor gold, nor wine,
Nor the rhythm of life is known.

MINERVA JONES

I am Minerva, the village poetess,
Hooted at, jeered at by the Yahoos of the street
For my heavy body, cock-eye, and rolling walk,
And all the more when "Butch" Weldy
Captured me after a brutal hunt.
He left me to my fate with Doctor Meyers;
And I sank into death, growing numb from the
    feet up,
Like one stepping deeper and deeper into a stream
    of ice.
Will some one go to the village newspaper,
And gather into a book the verses I wrote?—
I thirsted so for love!
I hungered so for life!

"INDIGNATION" JONES

You would not believe, would you,
That I came from good Welsh stock?
That I was purer blooded than the white trash
     here?
And of more direct lineage than the New
     Englanders
And Virginians of Spoon River?
You would not believe that I had been to school
And read some books.
You saw me only as a run-down man,
With matted hair and beard
And ragged clothes.
Sometimes a man's life turns into a cancer
From being bruised and continually bruised,
And swells into a purplish mass,
Like growths on stalks of corn.
Here was I, a carpenter, mired in a bog of life
Into which I walked, thinking it was a meadow,
With a slattern for a wife, and poor Minerva, my
     daughter,
Whom you tormented and drove to death.
So I crept, crept, like a snail through the days
Of my life.
No more you hear my footsteps in the morning,
Resounding on the hollow sidewalk,
Going to the grocery store for a little corn meal
And a nickel's worth of bacon.

DOCTOR MEYERS

No other man, unless it was Doc Hill,
Did more for people in this town than I.
And all the weak, the halt, the improvident
And those who could not pay flocked to me.
I was good-hearted, easy Doctor Meyers.
I was healthy, happy, in comfortable fortune,
Blest with a congenial mate, my children raised,
All wedded, doing well in the world.
And then one night, Minerva, the poetess,
Came to me in her trouble, crying.
I tried to help her out—she died—
They indicted me, the newspapers disgraced me,
My wife perished of a broken heart.
And pneumonia finished me.

MRS. MEYERS

He protested all his life long
The newspapers lied about him villainously;
That he was not at fault for Minerva's fall,
But only tried to help her.
Poor soul so sunk in sin he could not see
That even trying to help her, as he called it,
He had broken the law human and divine.
Passers by, an ancient admonition to you:
If your ways would be ways of pleasantness,
And all your pathways peace,*
Love God and keep his commandments.

---

*If your ways . . . peace *Proverbs* 3:17 (said of Wisdom personified)

"BUTCH" WELDY

After I got religion and steadied down
They gave me a job in the canning works,
And every morning I had to fill
The tank in the yard with gasoline,
That fed the blow-fires in the sheds
To heat the soldering irons.
And I mounted a rickety ladder to do it,
Carrying buckets full of the stuff.
One morning, as I stood there pouring,
The air grew still and seemed to heave,
And I shot up as the tank exploded,
And down I came with both legs broken,
And my eyes burned crisp as a couple of eggs
For someone left a blow-fire going,
And something sucked the flame in the tank.
The Circuit Judge said whoever did it
Was a fellow-servant of mine, and so
Old Rhodes' son didn't have to pay me.
And I sat on the witness stand as blind
As Jack the Fiddler, saying over and over,
"I didn't know him at all."

KNOWLT HOHEIMER

I was the first fruits of the battle of Missionary
    Ridge.
When I felt the bullet enter my heart
I wished I had staid at home and gone to jail
For stealing the hogs of Curl Trenary,
Instead of running away and joining the army.
Rather a thousand times the county jail
Than to lie under this marble figure with wings,
And this granite pedestal
Bearing the words, *"Pro Patria."**
What do they mean, anyway?

*"**Pro Patria.**" "for one's country," part of a longer familiar quota-
tion, "*Dulce et decorum est pro patria mori.*" (Horace, *Odes* III, 2. 13),
"It is sweet and honorable to die for one's country." There is a
strong irony here: Hoheimer doesn't know the Latin, or the famous
tag, so that he is as ignorant of the meaning of the unquoted part
as he is of the "meaning" of his death in the Civil War battle.
(See Introduction)

LYDIA PUCKETT

Knowlt Hoheimer ran away to the war
The day before Curl Trenary
Swore out a warrant through Justice Arnett
For stealing hogs.
But that's not the reason he turned a soldier.
He caught me running with Lucius Atherton.
We quarreled and I told him never again
To cross my path.
Then he stole the hogs and went to the war—
Back of every soldier is a woman.

FRANK DRUMMER

Out of a cell into this darkened space—
The end at twenty-five!
My tongue could not speak what stirred within
    me,
And the village thought me a fool.
Yet at the start there was a clear vision,
A high and urgent purpose in my soul
Which drove me on trying to memorize
The Encyclopedia Britannica!

HARE DRUMMER

Do the boys and girls still go to Siever's
For cider, after school, in late September?
Or gather hazel nuts among the thickets
On Aaron Hatfield's farm when the frosts begin?
For many times with the laughing girls and boys
Played I along the road and over the hills
When the sun was low and the air was cool,
Stopping to club the walnut tree
Standing leafless against a flaming west.
Now, the smell of the autumn smoke,
And the dropping acorns,
And the echoes about the vales
Bring dreams of life. They hover over me.
They question me:
Where are those laughing comrades?
How many are with me, how many
In the old orchards along the way to Siever's,
And in the woods that overlook
The quiet water?

CONRAD SIEVER

Not in that wasted garden
Where bodies are drawn into grass
That feeds no flocks, and into evergreens
That bear no fruit—
There where along the shaded walks
Vain sighs are heard,
And vainer dreams are dreamed
Of close communion with departed souls—
But here under the apple tree
I loved and watched and pruned
With gnarled hands
In the long, long years;
Here under the roots of this northern-spy*
To move in the chemic change and circle of life,
Into the soil and into the flesh of the tree,
And into the living epitaphs
Of redder apples!

*northern-spy** more properly, Northern Spy, a thin-skinned, juicy,
winter apple

DOC HILL

I went up and down the streets
Here and there by day and night,
Through all hours of the night caring for the poor
     who were sick.
Do you know why?
My wife hated me, my son went to the dogs.
And I turned to the people and poured out my
     love to them.
Sweet it was to see the crowds about the lawns
     on the day of my funeral,
And hear them murmur their love and sorrow.
But oh, dear God, my soul trembled, scarcely able
To hold to the railing of the new life
When I saw Em Stanton behind the oak tree
At the grave,
Hiding herself, and her grief!

ANDY THE NIGHT-WATCH

In my Spanish cloak,
And old slouch hat,
And overshoes of felt,
And Tyke, my faithful dog,
And my knotted hickory cane,
I slipped about with a bull's-eye lantern
From door to door on the square,
As the midnight stars wheeled round,
And the bell in the steeple murmured
From the blowing of the wind;
And the weary steps of old Doc Hill
Sounded like one who walks in sleep,
And a far-off rooster crew.
And now another is watching Spoon River
As others watched before me.
And here we lie, Doc Hill and I
Where none breaks through and steals,
And no eye needs to guard.

SARAH BROWN

Maurice, weep not, I am not here under this
    pine tree.
The balmy air of spring whispers through the
    sweet grass,
The stars sparkle, the whippoorwill calls,
But thou grievest, while my soul lies rapturous
In the blest Nirvana of eternal light!
Go to the good heart that is my husband,
Who broods upon what he calls our guilty love:—
Tell him that my love for you, no less than my
    love for him
Wrought out my destiny—that through the flesh
I won spirit, and through spirit, peace.
There is no marriage in heaven,*
But there is love.

*no marriage in heaven *Matthew* 22:3

PERCY BYSSHE SHELLEY

My father who owned the wagon-shop
And grew rich shoeing horses
Sent me to the University of Montreal.
I learned nothing and returned home,
Roaming the fields with Bert Kessler,
Hunting quail and snipe.
At Thompson's Lake the trigger of my gun
Caught in the side of the boat
And a great hole was shot through my heart.
Over me a fond father erected this marble shaft,
On which stands the figure of a woman
Carved by an Italian artist.
They say the ashes of my namesake
Were scattered near the pyramid of Caius Cestius
Somewhere near Rome.

FLOSSIE CABANIS

From Bindle's opera house in the village
To Broadway is a great step.
But I tried to take it, my ambition fired
When sixteen years of age,
Seeing "East Lynne" played here in the village
By Ralph Barrett, the coming
Romantic actor, who enthralled my soul.
True, I trailed back home, a broken failure,
When Ralph disappeared in New York,
Leaving me alone in the city—
But life broke him also.
In all this place of silence
There are no kindred spirits.
How I wish Duse could stand amid the pathos
Of these quiet fields
And read these words.

JULIA MILLER

We quarreled that morning,
For he was sixty-five, and I was thirty,
And I was nervous and heavy with the child
Whose birth I dreaded.
I thought over the last letter written me
By that estranged young soul
Whose betrayal of me I had concealed
By marrying the old man.
Then I took morphine and sat down to read.
Across the blackness that came over my eyes
I see the flickering light of these words even now:
"And Jesus said unto him, Verily
I say unto thee, To-day thou shalt
Be with me in paradise."*

*"And Jesus said . . . paradise" *Luke* 23:43

JOHNNIE SAYRE

Father, thou canst never know
The anguish that smote my heart
For my disobedience, the moment I felt
The remorseless wheel of the engine
Sink into the crying flesh of my leg.
As they carried me to the home of widow Morris
I could see the school-house in the valley
To which I played truant to steal rides upon the
    trains.
I prayed to live until I could ask your
    forgiveness—
And then your tears, your broken words of
    comfort!
From the solace of that hour I have gained infi-
    nite happiness.
Thou wert wise to chisel for me:
"Taken from the evil to come."

CHARLIE FRENCH

Did you ever find out
Which one of the O'Brien boys it was
Who snapped the toy pistol against my hand?
There when the flags were red and white
In the breeze and "Bucky" Estil
Was firing the cannon brought to Spoon River
From Vicksburg by Captain Harris;
And the lemonade stands were running
And the band was playing,
To have it all spoiled
By a piece of a cap shot under the skin of my
    hand,
And the boys all crowding about me saying:
"You'll die of lock-jaw, Charlie, sure."
Oh, dear! oh, dear!
What chum of mine could have done it?

ZENAS WITT

I was sixteen, and I had the most terrible dreams,
And specks before my eyes, and nervous
    weakness.
And I couldn't remember the books I read,
Like Frank Drummer who memorized page after
    page.
And my back was weak, and I worried and
    worried,
And I was embarrassed and stammered my
    lessons,
And when I stood up to recite I'd forget
Everything that I had studied.
Well, I saw Dr. Weese's advertisement,
And there I read everything in print,
Just as if he had known me;
And about the dreams which I couldn't help.
So I knew I was marked for an early grave.
And I worried until I had a cough,
And then the dreams stopped.
And then I slept the sleep without dreams
Here on the hill by the river.

THEODORE THE POET

As a boy, Theodore, you sat for long hours
On the shore of the turbid Spoon
With deep-set eye staring at the door of the craw-
     fish's burrow,
Waiting for him to appear, pushing ahead,
First his waving antennæ, like straws of hay,
And soon his body, colored like soap-stone,
Gemmed with eyes of jet.
And you wondered in a trance of thought
What he knew, what he desired, and why he lived
     at all.
But later your vision watched for men and women
Hiding in burrows of fate amid great cities,
Looking for the souls of them to come out,
So that you could see
How they lived, and for what,
And why they kept crawling so busily
Along the sandy way where water fails
As the summer wanes.

THE TOWN MARSHAL

The Prohibitionists made me Town Marshal
When the saloons were voted out,
Because when I was a drinking man,
Before I joined the church, I killed a Swede
At the saw-mill near Maple Grove.
And they wanted a terrible man,
Grim, righteous, strong, courageous,
And a hater of saloons and drinkers,
To keep law and order in the village.
And they presented me with a loaded cane
With which I struck Jack McGuire
Before he drew the gun with which he killed me.
The Prohibitionists spent their money in vain
To hang him, for in a dream
I appeared to one of the twelve jurymen
And told him the whole secret story.
Fourteen years were enough for killing me.

JACK McGUIRE

They would have lynched me
Had I not been secretly hurried away
To the jail at Peoria.
And yet I was going peacefully home,
Carrying my jug, a little drunk,
When Logan, the marshal, halted me,
Called me a drunken hound and shook me,
And, when I cursed him for it, struck me
With that Prohibition loaded cane—
All this before I shot him.
They would have hanged me except for this:
My lawyer, Kinsey Keene, was helping to land
Old Thomas Rhodes for wrecking the bank,
And the judge was a friend of Rhodes
And wanted him to escape,
And Kinsey offered to quit on Rhodes
For fourteen years for me.
And the bargain was made. I served my time
And learned to read and write.

DORCAS GUSTINE

I was not beloved of the villagers,
But all because I spoke my mind,
And met those who transgressed against me
With plain remonstrance, hiding nor nurturing
Nor secret griefs nor grudges.
That act of the Spartan boy is greatly praised,
Who hid the wolf under his cloak,
Letting it devour him, uncomplainingly.
It is braver, I think, to snatch the wolf forth
And fight him openly, even in the street,
Amid dust and howls of pain.
The tongue may be an unruly member—
But silence poisons the soul.
Berate me who will—I am content.

NICHOLAS BINDLE

Were you not ashamed, fellow citizens,
When my estate was probated and everyone knew
How small a fortune I left?—
You who hounded me in life,
To give, give, give to the churches, to the poor,
To the village!—me who had already given much.
And think you not I did not know
That the pipe-organ, which I gave to the church,
Played its christening songs when Deacon Rhodes,
Who broke the bank and all but ruined me,
Worshipped for the first time after his acquittal?

JACOB GOODPASTURE

When Fort Sumter fell and the war came
I cried out in bitterness of soul:
"O glorious republic now no more!"
When they buried my soldier son
To the call of trumpets and the sound of drums
My heart broke beneath the weight
Of eighty years, and I cried:
"Oh, son who died in a cause unjust!
In the strife of Freedom slain!"
And I crept here under the grass.
And now from the battlements of time, behold:
Thrice thirty million souls being bound together
In the love of larger truth,
Rapt in the expectation of the birth
Of a new Beauty,
Sprung from Brotherhood and Wisdom.
I with eyes of spirit see the Transfiguration
Before you see it.
But ye infinite brood of golden eagles nesting
        ever higher,
Wheeling ever higher, the sun-light wooing
Of lofty places of Thought,
Forgive the blindness of the departed owl.

HAROLD ARNETT

I leaned against the mantel, sick, sick,
Thinking of my failure, looking into the abysm,
Weak from the noon-day heat.
A church bell sounded mournfully far away,
I heard the cry of a baby,
And the coughing of John Yarnell,
Bed-ridden, feverish, feverish, dying,
Then the violent voice of my wife:
"Watch out, the potatoes are burning!"
I smelled them . . . then there was irresistible
    disgust.
I pulled the trigger . . . blackness . . . light . . .
Unspeakable regret . . . fumbling for the world
    again.
Too late! Thus I came here,
With lungs for breathing . . . one cannot breathe
    here with lungs,
Though one must breathe. . . . Of what use is it
To rid one's self of the world,
When no soul may ever escape the eternal destiny
    of life?

MARGARET FULLER SLACK

I would have been as great as George Eliot
But for an untoward fate.
For look at the photograph of me made by
     Penniwit,
Chin resting on hand, and deep-set eyes—
Gray, too, and far-searching.
But there was the old, old problem:
Should it be celibacy, matrimony or unchastity?
Then John Slack, the rich druggist, wooed me,
Luring me with the promise of leisure for my
     novel,
And I married him, giving birth to eight children,
And had no time to write.
It was all over with me, anyway,
When I ran the needle in my hand
While washing the baby's things,
And died from lock-jaw, an ironical death.
Hear me, ambitious souls,
Sex is the curse of life!

GEORGE TRIMBLE

Do you remember when I stood on the steps
Of the court-house and talked free-silver,
And the single-tax of Henry George?
Then do you remember that, when the Peerless
    Leader*
Lost the first battle, I began to talk prohibition,
And became active in the church?
That was due to my wife,
Who pictured to me my destruction
If I did not prove my morality to the people.
Well, she ruined me:
For the radicals grew suspicious of me,
And the conservatives were never sure of me—
And here I lie, unwept of all.

*Peerless Leader** William Jennings Bryan

DR. SIEGFRIED ISEMAN

I said when they handed me my diploma,
I said to myself I will be good
And wise and brave and helpful to others;
I said I will carry the Christian creed
Into the practice of medicine!
Somehow the world and the other doctors
Know what's in your heart as soon as you make
This high-souled resolution.
And the way of it is they starve you out.
And no one comes to you but the poor.
And you find too late that being a doctor
Is just a way of making a living.
And when you are poor and have to carry
The Christian creed and wife and children
All on your back, it is too much!
That's why I made the Elixir of Youth,
Which landed me in the jail at Peoria
Branded a swindler and a crook
By the upright Federal Judge!

"ACE" SHAW

I never saw any difference
Between playing cards for money
And selling real estate,
Practicing law, banking, or anything else.
For everything is chance.
Nevertheless
Seest thou a man diligent in business?
He shall stand before Kings!*

*Seest thou . . . Kings! *Proverbs* 22:29

LOIS SPEARS

Here lies the body of Lois Spears,
Born Lois Fluke, daughter of Willard Fluke,
Wife of Cyrus Spears,
Mother of Myrtle and Virgil Spears,
Children with clear eyes and sound limbs—
(I was born blind).
I was the happiest of women
As wife, mother and housekeeper,
Caring for my loved ones,
And making my home
A place of order and bounteous hospitality:
For I went about the rooms,
And about the garden
With an instinct as sure as sight,
As though there were eyes in my finger tips—
Glory to God in the highest.

JUSTICE ARNETT

It is true, fellow citizens,
That my old docket lying there for years
On a shelf above my head and over
The seat of justice, I say it is true
That docket had an iron rim
Which gashed my baldness when it fell—
(Somehow I think it was shaken loose
By the heave of the air all over town
When the gasoline tank at the canning works
Blew up and burned "Butch" Weldy)—
But let us argue points in order,
And reason the whole case carefully:
First I concede my head was cut,
But second the frightful thing was this:
The leaves of the docket shot and showered
Around me like a deck of cards
In the hands of a sleight of hand performer.
And up to the end I saw those leaves
Till I said at last, "Those are not leaves,
Why, can't you see they are days and days
And the days and days of seventy years?
And why do you torture me with leaves
And the little entries on them?"

WILLARD FLUKE

My wife lost her health,
And dwindled until she weighed scarce ninety
    pounds.
Then that woman, whom the men
Styled Cleopatra, came along.
And we—we married ones
All broke our vows, myself among the rest.
Years passed and one by one
Death claimed them all in some hideous form,
And I was borne along by dreams
Of God's particular grace for me,
And I began to write, write, write, reams on reams
Of the second coming of Christ.
Then Christ came to me and said,
"Go into the church and stand before the
    congregation
And confess your sin."
But just as I stood up and began to speak
I saw my little girl, who was sitting in the front
    seat—
My little girl who was born blind!*
After that, all is blackness!

*born blind presumably from congenital gonorrhea

ANER CLUTE

Over and over they used to ask me,
While buying the wine or the beer,
In Peoria first, and later in Chicago,
Denver, Frisco, New York, wherever I lived,
How I happened to lead the life,
And what was the start of it.
Well, I told them a silk dress,
And a promise of marriage from a rich man—
(It was Lucius Atherton).
But that was not really it at all.
Suppose a boy steals an apple
From the tray at the grocery store,
And they all begin to call him a thief,
The editor, minister, judge, and all the people—
"A thief," "a thief," "a thief," wherever he goes.
And he can't get work, and he can't get bread
Without stealing it, why the boy will steal.
It's the way the people regard the theft of the
     apple
That makes the boy what he is.

LUCIUS ATHERTON

When my moustache curled,
And my hair was black,
And I wore tight trousers
And a diamond stud,
I was an excellent knave of hearts and took many
    a trick.
But when the gray hairs began to appear—
Lo! a new generation of girls
Laughed at me, not fearing me,
And I had no more exciting adventures
Wherein I was all but shot for a heartless devil,
But only drabby affairs, warmed-over affairs
Of other days and other men.
And time went on until I lived at Mayer's
    restaurant,
Partaking of short-orders, a gray, untidy,
Toothless, discarded, rural Don Juan. . . .
There is a mighty shade here who sings
Of one named Beatrice;*
And I see now that the force that made him great
Drove me to the dregs of life.

*a mighty shade . . . Beatrice Dante Alighieri

HOMER CLAPP

Often Aner Clute at the gate
Refused me the parting kiss,
Saying we should be engaged before that;
And just with a distant clasp of the hand
She bade me good-night, as I brought her home
From the skating rink or the revival.
No sooner did my departing footsteps die away
Than Lucius Atherton,
(So I learned when Aner went to Peoria)
Stole in at her window, or took her riding
Behind his spanking team of bays
Into the country.
The shock of it made me settle down,
And I put all the money I got from my father's
    estate
Into the canning factory, to get the job
Of head accountant, and lost it all.
And then I knew I was one of Life's fools,
Whom only death would treat as the equal
Of other men, making me feel like a man.

DEACON TAYLOR

I belonged to the church,
And to the party of prohibition;
And the villagers thought I died of eating
    watermelon.
In truth I had cirrhosis of the liver,
For every noon for thirty years,
I slipped behind the prescription partition
In Trainor's drug store
And poured a generous drink
From the bottle marked
*"Spiritus frumenti."**

*"**Spiritus frumenti**" fermented spirits, i.e. grain alcohol in phar-
maceutical Latin

SAM HOOKEY

I ran away from home with the circus,
Having fallen in love with Mademoiselle
    Estralada,
The lion tamer.
One time, having starved the lions
For more than a day,
I entered the cage and began to beat Brutus
And Leo and Gypsy.
Whereupon Brutus sprang upon me,
And killed me.
On entering these regions
I met a shadow who cursed me,
And said it served me right. . . .
It was Robespierre!

COONEY POTTER

I inherited forty acres from my father
And, by working my wife, my two sons and two
     daughters
From dawn to dusk, I acquired
A thousand acres. But not content,
Wishing to own two thousand acres,
I bustled through the years with axe and plow,
Toiling, denying myself, my wife, my sons, my
     daughters.
Squire Higbee wrongs me to say
That I died from smoking Red Eagle cigars.
Eating hot pie and gulping coffee
During the scorching hours of harvest time
Brought me here ere I had reached my sixtieth
     year.

FIDDLER JONES

The earth keeps some vibration going
There in your heart, and that is you.
And if the people find you can fiddle,
Why, fiddle you must, for all your life.
What do you see, a harvest of clover?
Or a meadow to walk through to the river?
The wind's in the corn; you rub your hands
For beeves hereafter ready for market;
Or else you hear the rustle of skirts
Like the girls when dancing at Little Grove.
To Cooney Potter a pillar of dust
Or whirling leaves meant ruinous drouth;
They looked to me like Red-Head Sammy
Stepping it off, to "Toor-a-Loor."
How could I till my forty acres
Not to speak of getting more,
With a medley of horns, bassoons and piccolos
Stirred in my brain by crows and robins
And the creak of a wind-mill—only these?
And I never started to plow in my life
That some one did not stop in the road
And take me away to a dance or picnic.
I ended up with forty acres;
I ended up with a broken fiddle—
And a broken laugh, and a thousand memories.
And not a single regret.

NELLIE CLARK

I was only eight years old;
And before I grew up and knew what it meant
I had no words for it, except
That I was frightened and told my mother;
And that my father got a pistol
And would have killed Charlie, who was a big
      boy,
Fifteen years old, except for his mother.
Nevertheless the story clung to me.
But the man who married me, a widower of
      thirty-five,
Was a newcomer and never heard it
Till two years after we were married.
Then he considered himself cheated,
And the village agreed that I was not really a
      virgin.
Well, he deserted me, and I died
The following winter.

LOUISE SMITH

Herbert broke our engagement of eight years
When Annabelle returned to the village
From the Seminary, ah me!
If I had let my love for him alone
It might have grown into a beautiful sorrow—
Who knows?—filling my life with healing
    fragrance.
But I tortured it, I poisoned it,
I blinded its eyes, and it became hatred—
Deadly ivy instead of clematis.
And my soul fell from its support,
Its tendrils tangled in decay.
Do not let the will play gardener to your soul
Unless you are sure
It is wiser than your soul's nature.

HERBERT MARSHALL

All your sorrow, Louise, and hatred of me
Sprang from your delusion that it was wantonness
Of spirit and contempt of your soul's rights
Which made me turn to Annabelle and forsake
　　you.
You really grew to hate me for love of me,
Because I was your soul's happiness,
Formed and tempered
To solve your life for you, and would not.
But you were my misery. If you had been
My happiness would I not have clung to you?
This is life's sorrow:
That one can be happy only where two are;
And that our hearts are drawn to stars
Which want us not.

GEORGE GRAY

I have studied many times
The marble which was chiseled for me—
A boat with a furled sail at rest in a harbor.
In truth it pictures not my destination
But my life.
For love was offered me and I shrank from its
      disillusionment;
Sorrow knocked at my door, but I was afraid;
Ambition called to me, but I dreaded the chances.
Yet all the while I hungered for meaning in my
      life.
And now I know that we must lift the sail
And catch the winds of destiny
Wherever they drive the boat.
To put meaning in one's life may end in madness,
But life without meaning is the torture
Of restlessness and vague desire—
It is a boat longing for the sea and yet afraid.

HON. HENRY BENNETT

It never came into my mind
Until I was ready to die
That Jenny had loved me to death, with malice
    of heart.
For I was seventy, she was thirty-five,
And I wore myself to a shadow trying to husband
Jenny, rosy Jenny full of the ardor of life.
For all my wisdom and grace of mind
Gave her no delight at all, in very truth,
But ever and anon she spoke of the giant strength
Of Willard Shafer, and of his wonderful feat
Of lifting a traction engine out of the ditch
One time at Georgie Kirby's.
So Jenny inherited my fortune and married
    Willard—
That mount of brawn! That clownish soul!

GRIFFY THE COOPER

The cooper should know about tubs.
But I learned about life as well,
And you who loiter around these graves
Think you know life.
You think your eye sweeps about a wide hori-
    zon, perhaps,
In truth you are only looking around the interior
    of your tub.
You cannot lift yourself to its rim
And see the outer world of things,
And at the same time see yourself.
You are submerged in the tub of yourself—
Taboos and rules and appearances,
Are the staves of your tub.
Break them and dispel the witchcraft
Of thinking your tub is life!
And that you know life!

SEXSMITH THE DENTIST

Do you think that odes and sermons,
And the ringing of church bells,
And the blood of old men and young men,
Martyred for the truth they saw
With eyes made bright by faith in God,
Accomplished the world's great reformations?
Do you think that the Battle Hymn of the Republic
Would have been heard if the chattel slave
Had crowned the dominant dollar,
In spite of Whitney's cotton gin,
And steam and rolling mills and iron
And telegraphs and white free labor?
Do you think that Daisy Fraser
Had been put out and driven out
If the canning works had never needed
Her little house and lot?
Or do you think the poker room
Of Johnnie Taylor, and Burchard's bar
Had been closed up if the money lost
And spent for beer had not been turned,
By closing them, to Thomas Rhodes
For larger sales of shoes and blankets,
And children's cloaks and gold-oak cradles?
Why, a moral truth is a hollow tooth
Which must be propped with gold.

A. D. BLOOD

If you in the village think that my work was a
    good one,
Who closed the saloons and stopped all playing
    at cards,
And haled old Daisy Fraser before Justice Arnett,
In many a crusade to purge the people of sin;
Why do you let the milliner's daughter Dora,
And the worthless son of Benjamin Pantier
Nightly make my grave their unholy pillow?

ROBERT SOUTHEY BURKE

I spent my money trying to elect you Mayor,
A. D. Blood.
I lavished my admiration upon you,
You were to my mind the almost perfect man.
You devoured my personality,
And the idealism of my youth,
And the strength of a high-souled fealty.
And all my hopes for the world,
And all my beliefs in Truth,
Were smelted up in the blinding heat
Of my devotion to you,
And molded into your image.
And then when I found what you were:
That your soul was small
And your words were false
As your blue-white porcelain teeth,
And your cuffs of celluloid,
I hated the love I had for you,
I hated myself, I hated you
For my wasted soul, and wasted youth.
And I say to all, beware of ideals,
Beware of giving your love away
To any man alive.

DORA WILLIAMS

When Reuben Pantier ran away and threw me
I went to Springfield. There I met a lush,
Whose father just deceased left him a fortune.
He married me when drunk. My life was
    wretched.
A year passed and one day they found him dead.
That made me rich. I moved on to Chicago.
After a time met Tyler Rountree, villain.
I moved on to New York. A gray-haired magnate
Went mad about me—so another fortune.
He died one night right in my arms, you know.
(I saw his purple face for years thereafter.)
There was almost a scandal. I moved on,
This time to Paris. I was now a woman,
Insidious, subtle, versed in the world and rich.
My sweet apartment near the Champs Élysées
Became a center for all sorts of people,
Musicians, poets, dandies, artists, nobles,
Where we spoke French and German, Italian,
    English.
I wed Count Navigato, native of Genoa.
We went to Rome. He poisoned me, I think.
Now in the Campo Santo overlooking
The sea where young Columbus dreamed new
    worlds,
See what they chiseled: *"Contessa Navigato*
*Implora eterna quiete."**

---

*"*Contessa Navigato Implora eterna quiete*"* "Countess Navigato
asks for eternal peace"

MRS. WILLIAMS

I was the milliner
Talked about, lied about,
Mother of Dora,
Whose strange disappearance
Was charged to her rearing.
My eye quick to beauty
Saw much beside ribbons
And buckles and feathers
And leghorns and felts,
To set off sweet faces,
And dark hair and gold.
One thing I will tell you
And one I will ask:
The stealers of husbands
Wear powder and trinkets,
And fashionable hats.
Wives, wear them yourselves.
Hats may make divorces—
They also prevent them.
Well now, let me ask you:
If all of the children, born here in Spoon River
Had been reared by the County, somewhere on
        a farm;
And the fathers and mothers had been given
        their freedom
To live and enjoy, change mates if they wished,
Do you think that Spoon River
Had been any the worse?

WILLIAM AND EMILY

There is something about Death
Like love itself!
If with some one with whom you have known
        passion,
And the glow of youthful love,
You also, after years of life
Together, feel the sinking of the fire,
And thus fade away together,
Gradually, faintly, delicately,
As it were in each other's arms,
Passing from the familiar room—
That is a power of unison between souls
Like love itself!

THE CIRCUIT JUDGE

Take note, passers-by, of the sharp erosions
Eaten in my head-stone by the wind and rain—
Almost as if an intangible Nemesis or hatred
Were marking scores against me,
But to destroy, and not preserve, my memory.
I in life was the Circuit Judge, a maker of notches,
Deciding cases on the points the lawyers scored,
Not on the right of the matter.
O wind and rain, leave my head-stone alone!
For worse than the anger of the wronged,
The curses of the poor,
Was to lie speechless, yet with vision clear,
Seeing that even Hod Putt, the murderer,
Hanged by my sentence,
Was innocent in soul compared with me.

BLIND JACK

I had fiddled all day at the county fair.
But driving home "Butch" Weldy and Jack
      McGuire,
Who were roaring full, made me fiddle and fiddle
To the song of *Susie Skinner*, while whipping the
      horses
Till they ran away.
Blind as I was, I tried to get out
As the carriage fell in the ditch,
And was caught in the wheels and killed.
There's a blind man here with a brow
As big and white as a cloud.
And all we fiddlers, from highest to lowest,
Writers of music and tellers of stories,
Sit at his feet,
And hear him sing of the fall of Troy.

JOHN HORACE BURLESON

I won the prize essay at school
Here in the village,
And published a novel before I was twenty-five.
I went to the city for themes and to enrich my art;
There married the banker's daughter,
And later became president of the bank—
Always looking forward to some leisure
To write an epic novel of the war.
Meanwhile friend of the great, and lover of letters.
And host to Matthew Arnold and to Emerson.
An after dinner speaker, writing essays
For local clubs. At last brought here—
My boyhood home, you know—
Not even a little tablet in Chicago
To keep my name alive.
How great it is to write the single line:
"Roll on, thou deep and dark blue Ocean, roll!"*

*"Roll on, . . . roll!" Byron, *Childe Harold's Pilgrimage*, IV, 179

NANCY KNAPP

Well, don't you see this was the way of it:
We bought the farm with what he inherited,
And his brothers and sisters accused him of
    poisoning
His father's mind against the rest of them.
And we never had any peace with our treasure.
The murrain took the cattle, and the crops failed.
And lightning struck the granary.
So we mortgaged the farm to keep going.
And he grew silent and was worried all the time.
Then some of the neighbors refused to speak to us,
And took sides with his brothers and sisters.
And I had no place to turn, as one may say to
    himself,
At an earlier time in life; "No matter,
So and so is my friend, or I can shake this off
With a little trip to Decatur."
Then the dreadfulest smells infested the rooms.
So I set fire to the beds and the old witch-house
Went up in a roar of flame,
As I danced in the yard with waving arms,
While he wept like a freezing steer.

BARRY HOLDEN

The very fall my sister Nancy Knapp
Set fire to the house
They were trying Dr. Duval
For the murder of Zora Clemens,
And I sat in the court two weeks
Listening to every witness.
It was clear he had got her in a family way;
And to let the child be born
Would not do.
Well, how about me with eight children,
And one coming, and the farm
Mortgaged to Thomas Rhodes?
And when I got home that night,
(After listening to the story of the buggy ride,
And the finding of Zora in the ditch,)
The first thing I saw, right there by the steps,
Where the boys had hacked for angle worms,
Was the hatchet!
And just as I entered there was my wife,
Standing before me, big with child.
She started the talk of the mortgaged farm,
And I killed her.

STATE'S ATTORNEY FALLAS

I, the scourge-wielder, balance-wrecker,
Smiter with whips and swords;
I, hater of the breakers of the law;
I, legalist, inexorable and bitter,
Driving the jury to hang the madman, Barry
    Holden,
Was made as one dead by light too bright for eyes,
And woke to face a Truth with bloody brow:
Steel forceps fumbled by a doctor's hand
Against my boy's head as he entered life
Made him an idiot.
I turned to books of science
To care for him.
That's how the world of those whose minds are
    sick
Became my work in life, and all my world.
Poor ruined boy! You were, at last, the potter
And I and all my deeds of charity
The vessels of your hand.

WENDELL P. BLOYD

They first charged me with disorderly conduct,
There being no statute on blasphemy.
Later they locked me up as insane
Where I was beaten to death by a Catholic guard.
My offense was this:
I said God lied to Adam, and destined him
To lead the life of a fool,
Ignorant that there is evil in the world as well
    as good.
And when Adam outwitted God by eating the
    apple
And saw through the lie,
God drove him out of Eden to keep him from
    taking
The fruit of immortal life.
For Christ's sake, you sensible people,
Here's what God Himself says about it in the book
    of Genesis:
"And the Lord God said, behold the man
Is become as one of us" (a little envy, you see),
"To know good and evil" (The all-is-good lie
    exposed):
"And now lest he put forth his hand and take
Also of the tree of life and eat, and live forever:
Therefore the Lord God sent Him forth from the
    garden of Eden."
(The reason I believe God crucified His Own Son
To get out of the wretched tangle is, because it
    sounds just like Him.)

FRANCIS TURNER

I could not run or play
In boyhood.
In manhood I could only sip the cup,
Not drink—
For scarlet-fever left my heart diseased.
Yet I lie here
Soothed by a secret none but Mary knows:
There is a garden of acacia,
Catalpa trees, and arbors sweet with vines—
There on that afternoon in June
By Mary's side—
Kissing her with my soul upon my lips
It suddenly took flight.

FRANKLIN JONES

If I could have lived another year
I could have finished my flying machine,
And become rich and famous.
Hence it is fitting the workman
Who tried to chisel a dove for me
Made it look more like a chicken.
For what is it all but being hatched,
And running about the yard,
To the day of the block?
Save that a man has an angel's brain,
And sees the axe from the first!

JOHN M. CHURCH

I was attorney for the "Q"
And the Indemnity Company which insured
The owners of the mine.
I pulled the wires with judge and jury,
And the upper courts, to beat the claims
Of the crippled, the widow and orphan,
And made a fortune thereat.
The bar association sang my praises
In a high-flown resolution.
And the floral tributes were many—
But the rats devoured my heart
And a snake made a nest in my skull!

RUSSIAN SONIA

I, born in Weimar
Of a mother who was French
And German father, a most learned professor,
Orphaned at fourteen years,
Became a dancer, known as Russian Sonia,
All up and down the boulevards of Paris,
Mistress betimes of sundry dukes and counts,
And later of poor artists and of poets.
At forty years, *passée*, I sought New York
And met old Patrick Hummer on the boat,
Red-faced and hale, though turned his sixtieth
     year,
Returning after having sold a ship-load
Of cattle in the German city, Hamburg.
He brought me to Spoon River and we lived here
For twenty years—they thought that we were
     married!
This oak tree near me is the favorite haunt
Of blue jays chattering, chattering all the day.
And why not? for my very dust is laughing
For thinking of the humorous thing called life.

ISA NUTTER

Doc Meyers said I had satyriasis,
And Doc Hill called it leucæmia—
But I know what brought me here:
I was sixty-four but strong as a man
Of thirty-five or forty.
And it wasn't writing a letter a day,
And it wasn't late hours seven nights a week,
And it wasn't the strain of thinking of Minnie,
And it wasn't fear or a jealous dread,
Or the endless task of trying to fathom
Her wonderful mind, or sympathy
For the wretched life she led
With her first and second husband—
It was none of these that laid me low—
But the clamor of daughters and threats of sons,
And the sneers and curses of all my kin
Right up to the day I sneaked to Peoria
And married Minnie in spite of them—
And why do you wonder my will was made
For the best and purest of women?

BARNEY HAINSFEATHER

If the excursion train to Peoria
Had just been wrecked, I might have escaped with
    my life—
Certainly I should have escaped this place.
But as it was burned as well, they mistook me
For John Allen who was sent to the Hebrew
    Cemetery
At Chicago,
And John for me, so I lie here.
It was bad enough to run a clothing store in this
    town,
But to be buried here—*ach!*

PETIT THE POET

Seeds in a dry pod, tick, tick, tick,
Tick, tick, tick, like mites in a quarrel—
Faint iambics that the full breeze wakens—
But the pine tree makes a symphony thereof.
Triolets, villanelles, rondels, rondeaus,
Ballades* by the score with the same old thought:
The snows and the roses of yesterday† are vanished;
And what is love but a rose that fades?
Life all around me here in the village:
Tragedy, comedy, valor and truth,
Courage, constancy, heroism, failure—
All in the loom, and oh what patterns!
Woodlands, meadows, streams and rivers—
Blind to all of it all my life long.
Triolets, villanelles, rondels, rondeaus,
Seeds in a dry pod, tick, tick, tick,
Tick, tick, tick, what little iambics,
While Homer and Whitman roared in the pines?

*Triolets . . . Ballades** these are lyric forms, with complex patterns
of refrain, adapted from French poetry
†The snows . . . yesterday** an echo of the great French poet François Villon's famous ballade refrain, *"Ou sont les neiges d'antan,"*
"Where are the snows of yester-year?"

PAULINE BARRETT

Almost the shell of a woman after the surgeon's
      knife!
And almost a year to creep back into strength,
Till the dawn of our wedding decennial
Found me my seeming self again.
We walked the forest together,
By a path of soundless moss and turf.
But I could not look in your eyes,
And you could not look in my eyes,
For such sorrow was ours—the beginning of gray
      in your hair,
And I but a shell of myself.
And what did we talk of?—sky and water,
Anything, 'most, to hide our thoughts.
And then your gift of wild roses,
Set on the table to grace our dinner.
Poor heart, how bravely you struggled
To imagine and live a remembered rapture!
Then my spirit drooped as the night came on,
And you left me alone in my room for a while,
As you did when I was a bride, poor heart.
And I looked in the mirror and something said:
"One should be all dead when one is half-dead—
Nor ever mock life, nor ever cheat love."
And I did it looking there in the mirror—
Dear, have you ever understood?

MRS. CHARLES BLISS

Reverend Wiley advised me not to divorce him
For the sake of the children,
And Judge Somers advised him the same.
So we stuck to the end of the path.
But two of the children thought he was right,
And two of the children thought I was right.
And the two who sided with him blamed me,
And the two who sided with me blamed him,
And they grieved for the one they sided with.
And all were torn with the guilt of judging,
And tortured in soul because they could not
      admire
Equally him and me.
Now every gardener knows that plants grown in
      cellars
Or under stones are twisted and yellow and weak.
And no mother would let her baby suck
Diseased milk from her breast.
Yet preachers and judges advise the raising of
      souls
Where there is no sunlight, but only twilight,
No warmth, but only dampness and cold—
Preachers and judges!

MRS. GEORGE REECE

To this generation I would say:
Memorize some bit of verse of truth or beauty.
It may serve a turn in your life.
My husband had nothing to do
With the fall of the bank—he was only cashier.
The wreck was due to the president, Thomas
    Rhodes,
And his vain, unscrupulous son.
Yet my husband was sent to prison,
And I was left with the children,
To feed and clothe and school them.
And I did it, and sent them forth
Into the world all clean and strong,
And all through the wisdom of Pope, the poet:
"Act well your part, there all the honor lies."*

*"Act well . . . lies" Pope, *An Essay on Man*, IV, 194

REV. LEMUEL WILEY

I preached four thousand sermons,
I conducted forty revivals,
And baptized many converts.
Yet no deed of mine
Shines brighter in the memory of the world,
And none is treasured more by me:
Look how I saved the Blisses from divorce,
And kept the children free from that disgrace
To grow up into moral men and women,
Happy themselves, a credit to the village.

THOMAS ROSS, JR.

This I saw with my own eyes:
A cliff-swallow
Made her nest in a hole of the high clay-bank
There near Miller's Ford.
But no sooner were the young hatched
Than a snake crawled up to the nest
To devour the brood.
Then the mother swallow with swift flutterings
And shrill cries
Fought at the snake,
Blinding him with the beat of her wings,
Until he, wriggling and rearing his head,
Fell backward down the bank
Into Spoon River and was drowned.
Scarcely an hour passed
Until a shrike
Impaled the mother swallow on a thorn.
As for myself I overcame my lower nature
Only to be destroyed by my brother's ambition.

REV. ABNER PEET

I had no objection at all
To selling my household effects at auction
On the village square.
It gave my beloved flock the chance
To get something which had belonged to me
For a memorial.
But that trunk which was struck off
To Burchard, the grog-keeper!
Did you know it contained the manuscripts
Of a lifetime of sermons?
And he burned them as waste paper.

JEFFERSON HOWARD

My valiant fight! For I call it valiant,
With my father's beliefs from old Virginia:
Hating slavery, but no less war.
I, full of spirit, audacity, courage
Thrown into life here in Spoon River,
With its dominant forces drawn from New
    England,
Republicans, Calvinists, merchants, bankers,
Hating me, yet fearing my arm.
With wife and children heavy to carry—
Yet fruits of my very zest of life.
Stealing odd pleasures that cost me prestige,
And reaping evils I had not sown;
Foe of the church with its charnel dankness,
Friend of the human touch of the tavern;
Tangled with fates all alien to me,
Deserted by hands I called my own.
Then just as I felt my giant strength
Short of breath, behold my children
Had wound their lives in stranger gardens—
And I stood alone, as I started alone!
My valiant life! I died on my feet,
Facing the silence—facing the prospect
That no one would know of the fight I made.

JUDGE SELAH LIVELY

Suppose you stood just five feet two,
And had worked your way as a grocery clerk,
Studying law by candle light
Until you became an attorney at law?
And then suppose through your diligence,
And regular church attendance,
You became attorney for Thomas Rhodes,
Collecting notes and mortgages,
And representing all the widows
In the Probate Court? And through it all
They jeered at your size, and laughed at your
      clothes
And your polished boots? And then suppose
You became the County Judge?
And Jefferson Howard and Kinsey Keene,
And Harmon Whitney, and all the giants
Who had sneered at you, were forced to stand
Before the bar and say "Your Honor"—
Well, don't you think it was natural
That I made it hard for them?

ALBERT SCHIRDING

Jonas Keene thought his lot a hard one
Because his children were all failures.
But I know of a fate more trying than that:
It is to be a failure while your children are
    successes.
For I raised a brood of eagles
Who flew away at last, leaving me
A crow on the abandoned bough.
Then, with the ambition to prefix Honorable to
    my name,
And thus to win my children's admiration,
I ran for County Superintendent of Schools,
Spending my accumulations to win—and lost.
That fall my daughter received first prize in Paris
For her picture, entitled, "The Old Mill"—
(It was of the water mill before Henry Wilkin put
    in steam.)
The feeling that I was not worthy of her finished
    me.

JONAS KEENE

Why did Albert Schirding kill himself
Trying to be County Superintendent of Schools,
Blest as he was with the means of life
And wonderful children, bringing him honor
Ere he was sixty?
If even one of my boys could have run a news-
      stand,
Or one of my girls could have married a decent
      man,
I should not have walked in the rain
And jumped into bed with clothes all wet,
Refusing medical aid.

EUGENIA TODD

Have any of you, passers-by,
Had an old tooth that was an unceasing
    discomfort?
Or a pain in the side that never quite left you?
Or a malignant growth that grew with time?
So that even in profoundest slumber
There was shadowy consciousness or the phantom
    of thought
Of the tooth, the side, the growth?
Even so thwarted love, or defeated ambition,
Or a blunder in life which mixed your life
Hopelessly to the end,
Will, like a tooth, or a pain in the side,
Float through your dreams in the final sleep
Till perfect freedom from the earth-sphere
Comes to you as one who wakes
Healed and glad in the morning!

YEE BOW

They got me into the Sunday school
In Spoon River
And tried to get me to drop Confucius for Jesus.
I could have been no worse off
If I had tried to get them to drop Jesus for
      Confucius.
For, without any warning, as if it were a prank,
And sneaking up behind me, Harry Wiley,
The minister's son, caved my ribs into my lungs,
With a blow of his fist.
Now I shall never sleep with my ancestors in
      Pekin,
And no children shall worship at my grave.

WASHINGTON McNEELY

Rich, honored by my fellow citizens,
The father of many children, born of a noble mother,
All raised there
In the great mansion-house, at the edge of town.
Note the cedar tree on the lawn!
I sent all the boys to Ann Arbor, all the girls to
        Rockford,
The while my life went on, getting more riches
        and honors—
Resting under my cedar tree at evening.
The years went on.
I sent the girls to Europe;
I dowered them when married.
I gave the boys money to start in business.
They were strong children, promising as apples
Before the bitten places show.
But John fled the country in disgrace.
Jenny died in child-birth—
I sat under my cedar tree.
Harry killed himself after a debauch,
Susan was divorced—
I sat under my cedar tree.
Paul was invalided from over study,
Mary became a recluse at home for love of a man—
I sat under my cedar tree.
All were gone, or broken-winged or devoured by
        life—
I sat under my cedar tree.
My mate, the mother of them, was taken—
I sat under my cedar tree.
Till ninety years were tolled.
O maternal Earth, which rocks the fallen leaf to
        sleep!

PAUL McNEELY

Dear Jane! dear winsome Jane!
How you stole in the room (where I lay so ill)
In your nurse's cap and linen cuffs,
And took my hand and said with a smile:
"You are not so ill—you'll soon be well."
And how the liquid thought of your eyes
Sank in my eyes like dew that slips
Into the heart of a flower.
Dear Jane! the whole McNeely fortune
Could not have bought your care of me,
By day and night, and night and day;
Nor paid for your smile, nor the warmth of your
     soul,
In your little hands laid on my brow.
Jane, till the flame of life went out
In the dark above the disk of night
I longed and hoped to be well again
To pillow my head on your little breasts,
And hold you fast in a clasp of love—
Did my father provide for you when he died,
Jane, dear Jane?

MARY McNEELY

Passer-by,
To love is to find your own soul
Through the soul of the beloved one.
When the beloved one withdraws itself from
      your soul
Then you have lost your soul.
It is written: "I have a friend,
But my sorrow has no friend."
Hence my long years of solitude at the home of
      my father,
Trying to get myself back,
And to turn my sorrow into a supremer self.
But there was my father with his sorrows,
Sitting under the cedar tree,
A picture that sank into my heart at last
Bringing infinite repose.
Oh, ye souls who have made life
Fragrant and white as tube roses
From earth's dark soil,
Eternal peace!

DANIEL M'CUMBER

When I went to the city, Mary McNeely,
I meant to return for you, yes I did.
But Laura, my landlady's daughter,
Stole into my life somehow, and won me away.
Then after some years whom should I meet
But Georgine Miner from Niles—a sprout
Of the free love, Fourierist* gardens that flourished
Before the war all over Ohio.
Her dilettante lover had tired of her,
And she turned to me for strength and solace.
She was some kind of a crying thing
One takes in one's arms, and all at once
It slimes your face with its running nose,
And voids its essence all over you;
Then bites your hand and springs away.
And there you stand bleeding and smelling to
     heaven!
Why, Mary McNeely, I was not worthy
To kiss the hem of your robe!

---

*Fourierist** François Marie Charles Fourier (1772–1837), French so-
cialist and author of plans for Utopian communes, some of which
were started in the American Mid-west

GEORGINE SAND MINER

A step-mother drove me from home, embittering me.
A squaw-man, a flaneur and dilettante took my
    virtue.
For years I was his mistress—no one knew.
I learned from him the parasite cunning
With which I moved with the bluffs, like a flea on
    a dog.
All the time I was nothing but "very private" with
    different men.
Then Daniel, the radical, had me for years.
His sister called me his mistress;
And Daniel wrote me: "Shameful word, soiling
    our beautiful love!"
But my anger coiled, preparing its fangs.
My Lesbian friend next took a hand.
She hated Daniel's sister.
And Daniel despised her midget husband.
And she saw a chance for a poisonous thrust:
I must complain to the wife of Daniel's pursuit!
But before I did that I begged him to fly to London
    with me.
"Why not stay in the city just as we have?" he
    asked.
Then I turned submarine and revenged his repulse
In the arms of my dilettante friend. Then up to
    the surface,
Bearing the letter that Daniel wrote me,
To prove my honor was all intact, showing it to
    his wife,
My Lesbian friend and everyone.
If Daniel had only shot me dead!
Instead of stripping me naked of lies,
A harlot in body and soul!

THOMAS RHODES

Very well, you liberals,
And navigators into realms intellectual,
You sailors through heights imaginative,
Blown about my erratic currents, tumbling into
     air pockets,
You Margaret Fuller Slacks, Petits,
And Tennessee Claflin Shopes—
You found with all your boasted wisdom
How hard at the last it is
To keep the soul from splitting into cellular atoms.
While we, seekers of earth's treasures,
Getters and hoarders of gold,
Are self-contained, compact, harmonized,
Even to the end.

IDA CHICKEN

After I had attended lectures
At our Chautauqua, and studied French
For twenty years, committing the grammar
Almost by heart,
I thought I'd take a trip to Paris
To give my culture a final polish.
So I went to Peoria for a passport—
(Thomas Rhodes was on the train that morning.)
And there the clerk of the district Court
Made me swear to support and defend
The constitution—yes, even me—
Who couldn't defend or support it at all!
And what do you think? That very morning
The Federal Judge, in the very next room
To the room where I took the oath,
Decided the constitution
Exempted Rhodes from paying taxes
For the water works of Spoon River!

PENNIWIT THE ARTIST

I lost my patronage in Spoon River
From trying to put my mind in the camera
To catch the soul of the person.
The very best picture I ever took
Was of Judge Somers, attorney at law.
He sat upright and had me pause
Till he got his cross-eye straight.
Then when he was ready he said "all right."
And I yelled "overruled" and his eye turned up.
And I caught him just as he used to look
When saying "I except."

JIM BROWN

While I was handling Dom Pedro
I got at the thing that divides the race between
     men who are
For singing "Turkey in the straw" or "There is a
     fountain filled with blood"—
(Like Rile Potter used to sing it over at Concord);
For cards, or for Rev. Peet's lecture on the holy
     land;
For skipping the light fantastic, or passing the
     plate;
For Pinafore, or a Sunday school cantata;
For men, or for money;
For the people or against them.
This was it:
Rev. Peet and the Social Purity Club,
Headed by Ben Pantier's wife,
Went to the village trustees,
And asked them to make me take Dom Pedro
From the barn of Wash McNeely, there at the edge
     of town,
To a barn outside of the corporation,
On the ground that it corrupted public morals.
Well, Ben Pantier and Fiddler Jones saved the
     day—
They thought it a slam on colts.

ROBERT DAVIDSON

I grew spiritually fat living off the souls of men.
If I saw a soul that was strong
I wounded its pride and devoured its strength.
The shelters of friendship knew my cunning,
For where I could steal a friend I did so.
And wherever I could enlarge my power
By undermining ambition, I did so,
Thus to make smooth my own.
And to triumph over other souls,
Just to assert and prove my superior strength,
Was with me a delight,
The keen exhilaration of soul gymnastics.
Devouring souls, I should have lived forever.
But their undigested remains bred in me a
    deadly nephritis,
With fear, restlessness, sinking spirits,
Hatred, suspicion, vision disturbed.
I collapsed at last with a shriek.
Remember the acorn;
It does not devour other acorns.

ELSA WERTMAN

I was a peasant girl from Germany,
Blue-eyed, rosy, happy and strong.
And the first place I worked was at Thomas
     Greene's.
On a summer's day when she was away
He stole into the kitchen and took me
Right in his arms and kissed me on my throat,
I turning my head. Then neither of us
Seemed to know what happened.
And I cried for what would become of me.
And cried and cried as my secret began to show.
One day Mrs. Greene said she understood,
And would make no trouble for me,
And, being childless, would adopt it.
(He had given her a farm to be still.)
So she hid in the house and sent out rumors,
As if it were going to happen to her.
And all went well and the child was born—They
     were so kind to me.
Later I married Gus Wertman, and years passed.
But—at political rallies when sitters-by thought I
     was crying
At the eloquence of Hamilton Greene—
That was not it.
No! I wanted to say:
That's my son! That's my son!

HAMILTON GREENE

I was the only child of Frances Harris of Virginia
And Thomas Greene of Kentucky,
Of valiant and honorable blood both.
To them I owe all that I became,
Judge, member of Congress, leader in the State.
From my mother I inherited
Vivacity, fancy, language;
From my father will, judgment, logic.
All honor to them
For what service I was to the people!

ERNEST HYDE

My mind was a mirror:
It saw what it saw, it knew what it knew.
In youth my mind was just a mirror
In a rapidly flying car,
Which catches and loses bits of the landscape.
Then in time
Great scratches were made on the mirror,
Letting the outside world come in,
And letting my inner self look out.
For this is the birth of the soul in sorrow,
A birth with gains and losses.
The mind sees the world as a thing apart,
And the soul makes the world at one with itself.
A mirror scratched reflects no image—
And this is the silence of wisdom.

ROGER HESTON

Oh many times did Ernest Hyde and I
Argue about the freedom of the will.
My favorite metaphor was Prickett's cow
Roped out to grass, and free you know as far
As the length of the rope.
One day while arguing so, watching the cow
Pull at the rope to get beyond the circle
Which she had eaten bare,
Out came the stake, and tossing up her head,
She ran for us.
"What's that, free-will or what?" said Ernest,
        running.
I fell just as she gored me to my death.

AMOS SIBLEY

Not character, not fortitude, not patience
Were mine, the which the village thought I had
In bearing with my wife, while preaching on,
Doing the work God chose for me.
I loathed her as a termagant, as a wanton.
I knew of her adulteries, every one.
But even so, if I divorced the woman
I must forsake the ministry.
Therefore to do God's work and have it crop,
I bore with her!
So lied I to myself!
So lied I to Spoon River!
Yet I tried lecturing, ran for the legislature,
Canvassed for books, with just the thought in
    mind:
If I make money thus, I will divorce her.

MRS. SIBLEY

The secret of the stars,—gravitation.
The secret of the earth,—layers of rock.
The secret of the soil,—to receive seed.
The secret of the seed,—the germ.
The secret of man,—the sower.
The secret of woman,—the soil.
My secret: Under a mound that you shall never
    find.

ADAM WEIRAUCH

I was crushed between Altgeld and Armour.*
I lost many friends, much time and money
Fighting for Altgeld whom Editor Whedon
Denounced as the candidate of gamblers and
    anarchists.
Then Armour started to ship dressed meat to
    Spoon River,
Forcing me to shut down my slaughter-house,
And my butcher shop went all to pieces.
The new forces of Altgeld and Armour caught me
At the same time.
I thought it due me, to recoup the money I lost
And to make good the friends that left me,
For the Governor to appoint me Canal
    Commissioner.
Instead he appointed Whedon of the Spoon
    River *Argus*,
So I ran for the legislature and was elected.
I said to hell with principle and sold my vote
On Charles T. Yerkes' street-car franchise.
Of course I was one of the fellows they caught.
Who was it, Armour, Altgeld or myself
That ruined me?

***Altgeld and Armour** John Peter Altgeld (1847–1902), radical re-
former and governor of Illinois, 1892–1896; Philip Danforth Armour (1832–1901), meat packer, grain dealer, financier; he was
powerful and philanthropic and opposed to organized labor

EZRA BARTLETT

A chaplain in the army,
A chaplain in the prisons,
An exhorter in Spoon River,
Drunk with divinity, Spoon River—
Yet bringing poor Eliza Johnson to shame,
And myself to scorn and wretchedness.
But why will you never see that love of women,
And even love of wine,
Are the stimulants by which the soul, hungering
    for divinity,
Reaches the ecstatic vision
And sees the celestial outposts?
Only after many trials for strength,
Only when all stimulants fail,
Does the aspiring soul
By its own sheer power
Find the divine
By resting upon itself.

AMELIA GARRICK

Yes, here I lie close to a stunted rose bush
In a forgotten place near the fence
Where the thickets from Siever's woods
Have crept over, growing sparsely.
And you, you are a leader in New York,
The wife of a noted millionaire,
A name in the society columns,
Beautiful, admired, magnified perhaps
By the mirage of distance.
You have succeeded, I have failed
In the eyes of the world.
You are alive, I am dead.
Yet I know that I vanquished your spirit;
And I know that lying here far from you,
Unheard of among your great friends
In the brilliant world where you move,
I am really the unconquerable power over your
    life
That robs it of complete triumph.

JOHN HANCOCK OTIS

As to democracy, fellow citizens,
Are you not prepared to admit
That I, who inherited riches and was to the man-
    ner born,
Was second to none in Spoon River
In my devotion to the cause of Liberty?
While my contemporary, Anthony Findlay,
Born in a shanty and beginning life
As a water carrier to the section hands,
Then becoming a section hand when he was
    grown,
Afterwards foreman of the gang, until he rose
To the superintendency of the railroad,
Living in Chicago,
Was a veritable slave driver,
Grinding the faces of labor,
And a bitter enemy of democracy.
And I say to you, Spoon River,
And to you, O republic,
Beware of the man who rises to power
From one suspender.

ANTHONY FINDLAY

Both for the country and for the man,
And for a country as well as a man,
'Tis better to be feared than loved.
And if this country would rather part
With the friendship of every nation
Than surrender its wealth,
I say of a man 'tis worse to lose
Money than friends.
And I rend the curtain that hides the soul
Of an ancient aspiration:
When the people clamor for freedom
They really seek for power o'er the strong.
I, Anthony Findlay, rising to greatness
From a humble water carrier,
Until I could say to thousands "Come,"
And say to thousands "Go,"
Affirm that a nation can never be good,
Or achieve the good,
Where the strong and the wise have not the rod
To use on the dull and weak.

JOHN CABANIS

Neither spite, fellow citizens,
Nor forgetfulness of the shiftlessness,
And the lawlessness and waste
Under democracy's rule in Spoon River
Made me desert the party of law and order
And lead the liberal party.
Fellow citizens! I saw as one with second sight
That every man of the millions of men
Who give themselves to Freedom,
And fail while Freedom fails,
Enduring waste and lawlessness,
And the rule of the weak and the blind,
Dies in the hope of building earth,
Like the coral insect, for the temple
To stand on at the last.
And I swear that Freedom will wage to the end
The war for making every soul
Wise and strong and as fit to rule
As Plato's lofty guardians*
In a world republic girdled!

---

*Plato's lofty guardians the elite philosopher-kings of Plato's *Republic*

THE UNKNOWN

Ye aspiring ones, listen to the story of the
     unknown
Who lies here with no stone to mark the place.
As a boy reckless and wanton,
Wandering with gun in hand through the forest
Near the mansion of Aaron Hatfield,
I shot a hawk perched on the top
Of a dead tree.
He fell with guttural cry
At my feet, his wing broken.
Then I put him in a cage
Where he lived many days cawing angrily at me
When I offered him food.
Daily I search the realms of Hades
For the soul of the hawk,
That I may offer him the friendship
Of one whom life wounded and caged.

ALEXANDER THROCKMORTON

In youth my wings were strong and tireless,
But I did not know the mountains.
In age I knew the mountains
But my weary wings could not follow my vision—
Genius is wisdom and youth.

JONATHAN SWIFT SOMERS*

After you have enriched your soul
To the highest point,
With books, thought, suffering, the understanding
    of many personalities,
The power to interpret glances, silences,
The pauses in momentous transformations,
The genius of divination and prophecy;
So that you feel able at times to hold the world
In the hollow of your hand;
Then, if, by the crowding of so many powers
Into the compass of your soul,
Your soul takes fire,
And in the conflagration of your soul
The evil of the world is lighted up and made
    clear—
Be thankful if in that hour of supreme vision
Life does not fiddle.

*Author of THE SPOONIAD—see page 265.

WIDOW McFARLANE

I was the Widow McFarlane,
Weaver of carpets for all the village.
And I pity you still at the loom of life,
You who are singing to the shuttle
And lovingly watching the work of your hands,
If you reach the day of hate, of terrible truth.
For the cloth of life is woven, you know,
To a pattern hidden under the loom—
A pattern you never see!
And you weave high-hearted, singing, singing,
You guard the threads of love and friendship
For noble figures in gold and purple.
And long after other eyes can see
You have woven a moon-white strip of cloth,
You laugh in your strength, for Hope o'erlays it
With shapes of love and beauty.
The loom stops short! The pattern's out!
You're alone in the room! You have woven a
    shroud!
And hate of it lays you in it!

CARL HAMBLIN

The press of the Spoon River *Clarion* was wrecked,
And I was tarred and feathered,
For publishing this on the day the Anarchists*
    were hanged in Chicago:
"I saw a beautiful woman with bandaged eyes
Standing on the steps of a marble temple.
Great multitudes passed in front of her,
Lifting their faces to her imploringly.
In her left hand she held a sword.
She was brandishing the sword,
Sometimes striking a child, again a laborer,
Again a slinking woman, again a lunatic.
In her right hand she held a scale;
Into the scale pieces of gold were tossed
By those who dodged the strokes of the sword.
A man in a black gown read from a manuscript:
'She is no respecter of persons.'
Then a youth wearing a red cap
Leaped to her side and snatched away the
    bandage.
And lo, the lashes had been eaten away
From the oozy eye-lids;
The eye-balls were seared with a milky mucus;
The madness of a dying soul
Was written on her face—
But the multitude saw why she wore the
    bandage."

*Anarchists in the Haymarket Riot in Chicago (1886), a bomb was
thrown during a mass protest against the killing of strikers by the
police; several anarcho-syndicalists were arrested, and although
some were pardoned by Governor Altgeld (see note, p. 126), four
were eventually executed.

EDITOR WHEDON

To be able to see every side of every question;
To be on every side, to be everything, to be noth-
    ing long;
To pervert truth, to ride it for a purpose,
To use great feelings and passions of the human
    family
For base designs, for cunning ends,
To wear a mask like the Greek actors—
Your eight-page paper—behind which you
    huddle,
Bawling through the megaphone of big type:
"This is I, the giant."
Thereby also living the life of a sneak-thief,
Poisoned with the anonymous words
Of your clandestine soul.
To scratch dirt over scandal for money,
And exhume it to the winds for revenge,
Or to sell papers,
Crushing reputations, or bodies, if need be,
To win at any cost, save your own life.
To glory in demoniac power, ditching civilization,
As a paranoiac boy puts a log on the track
And derails the express train.
To be an editor, as I was.
Then to lie here close by the river over the place
Where the sewage flows from the village,
And the empty cans and garbage are dumped,
And abortions are hidden.

EUGENE CARMAN

Rhodes' slave! Selling shoes and gingham,
Flour and bacon, overalls, clothing, all day long
For fourteen hours a day for three hundred and
    thirteen days
For more than twenty years.
Saying "Yes'm" and "Yes, sir" and "Thank you"
A thousand times a day, and all for fifty dollars
    a month.
Living in this stinking room in the rattle-trap
    "Commercial."
And compelled to go to Sunday school, and to
    listen
To the Rev. Abner Peet one hundred and four
    times a year
For more than an hour at a time,
Because Thomas Rhodes ran the church
As well as the store and the bank.
So while I was tying my neck-tie that morning
I suddenly saw myself in the glass:
My hair all gray, my face like a sodden pie.
So I cursed and cursed: You damned old thing!
You cowardly dog! You rotten pauper!
You Rhodes slave! Till Roger Baughman
Thought I was having a fight with some one,
And looked through the transom just in time
To see me fall on the floor in a heap
From a broken vein in my head.

CLARENCE FAWCETT

The sudden death of Eugene Carman
Put me in line to be promoted to fifty dollars a
     month,
And I told my wife and children that night.
But it didn't come, and so I thought
Old Rhodes suspected me of stealing
The blankets I took and sold on the side
For money to pay a doctor's bill for my little girl.
Then like a bolt old Rhodes accused me,
And promised me mercy for my family's sake
If I confessed, and so I confessed,
And begged him to keep it out of the papers,
And I asked the editors, too.
That night at home the constable took me
And every paper, except the *Clarion*,
Wrote me up as a thief
Because old Rhodes was an advertiser
And wanted to make an example of me.
Oh! well, you know how the children cried,
And how my wife pitied and hated me,
And how I came to lie here.

W. LLOYD GARRISON STANDARD*

Vegetarian, non-resistant, free-thinker, in ethics a
    Christian;
Orator apt at the rhine-stone rhythm of Ingersoll;†
Carnivorous, avenger, believer and pagan;
Continent, promiscuous, changeable, treacherous,
    vain,
Proud, with the pride that makes struggle a thing
    for laughter;
With heart cored out by the worm of theatric
    despair;
Wearing the coat of indifference to hide the shame
    of defeat;
I, child of the abolitionist idealism—
A sort of *Brand*‡ in a birth of half-and-half.
What other thing could happen when I defended
The patriot scamps who burned the court-house,
That Spoon River might have a new one,
Than plead them guilty? When Kinsey Keene
    drove through
The card-board mask of my life with a spear of
    light,
What could I do but slink away, like the beast
    of myself
Which I raised from a whelp, to a corner and
    growl.
The pyramid of my life was nought but a dune,
Barren and formless, spoiled at last by the storm.

---

*William Lloyd Garrison (1805–1879), a bold, passionate and un-
compromising abolitionist
†Ingersoll Robert Green Ingersoll (1833–1899), Illinois lawyer and
politician, most famous for his agnostic lecturing and preaching
‡Brand Ibsen's play about a young clergyman whose uncompromis-
ing ethical principle of "all or nothing" led him to spiritual crisis

PROFESSOR NEWCOMER

Everyone laughed at Col. Prichard
For buying an engine so powerful
That it wrecked itself, and wrecked the grinder
He ran it with.
But here is a joke of cosmic size:
The urge of nature that made a man
Evolve from his brain a spiritual life—
Oh miracle of the world!—
The very same brain with which the ape and wolf
Get food and shelter and procreate themselves.
Nature has made man do this,
In a world where she gives him nothing to do
After all—(though the strength of his soul goes
        round
In a futile waste of power,
To gear itself to the mills of the gods)—
But get food and shelter and procreate himself!

RALPH RHODES

All they said was true:
I wrecked my father's bank with my loans
To dabble in wheat; but this was true—
I was buying wheat for him as well,
Who couldn't margin the deal in his name
Because of his church relationship.
And while George Reece was serving his term
I chased the will-o'-the-wisp of women,
And the mockery of wine in New York.
It's deathly to sicken of wine and women
When nothing else is left in life.
But suppose your head is gray, and bowed
On a table covered with acrid stubs
Of cigarettes and empty glasses,
And a knock is heard, and you know it's the knock
So long drowned out by popping corks
And the pea-cock screams of demireps—*
And you look up, and there's your Theft,
Who waited until your head was gray,
And your heart skipped beats to say to you:
The game is ended. I've called for you,
Go out on Broadway and be run over,
They'll ship you back to Spoon River.

*demireps whores

MICKEY M'GREW

It was just like everything else in life:
Something outside myself drew me down,
My own strength never failed me.
Why, there was the time I earned the money
With which to go away to school,
And my father suddenly needed help
And I had to give him all of it.
Just so it went till I ended up
A man-of-all-work in Spoon River.
Thus when I got the water-tower cleaned,
And they hauled me up the seventy feet,
I unhooked the rope from my waist,
And laughingly flung my giant arms
Over the smooth steel lips of the top of the
    tower—
But they slipped from the treacherous slime,
And down, down, down, I plunged
Through bellowing darkness!

ROSIE ROBERTS

I was sick, but more than that, I was mad
At the crooked police, and the crooked game of
    life
So I wrote to the Chief of Police at Peoria:
"I am here in my girlhood home in Spoon River,
Gradually wasting away.
But come and take me, I killed the son
Of the merchant prince, in Madam Lou's,
And the papers that said he killed himself
In his home while cleaning a hunting gun—
Lied like the devil to hush up scandal,
For the bribe of advertising.
In my room I shot him, at Madam Lou's,
Because he knocked me down when I said
That, in spite of all the money he had,
I'd see my lover that night."

OSCAR HUMMEL

I staggered on through darkness,
There was a hazy sky, a few stars
Which I followed as best I could.
It was nine o'clock, I was trying to get home.
But somehow I was lost,
Though really keeping the road.
Then I reeled through a gate and into a yard,
And called at the top of my voice:
"Oh, Fiddler! Oh, Mr. Jones!"
(I thought it was his house and he would show
     me the way home.)
But who should step out but A. D. Blood,
In his night shirt, waving a stick of wood,
And roaring about the cursed saloons,
And the criminals they made?
"You drunken Oscar Hummel," he said,
As I stood there weaving to and fro,
Taking the blows from the stick in his hand
Till I dropped down dead at his feet.

ROSCOE PURKAPILE

She loved me. Oh! how she loved me!
I never had a chance to escape
From the day she first saw me.
But then after we were married I thought
She might prove her mortality and let me out,
Or she might divorce me.
But few die, none resign.
Then I ran away and was gone a year on a lark.
But she never complained. She said all would be
     well,
That I would return. And I did return.
I told her that while taking a row in a boat
I had been captured near Van Buren Street
By pirates on Lake Michigan,
And kept in chains, so I could not write her.
She cried and kissed me, and said it was cruel,
Outrageous, inhuman!
I then concluded our marriage
Was a divine dispensation
And could not be dissolved,
Except by death.
I was right.

MRS. PURKAPILE

He ran away and was gone for a year.
When he came home he told me the silly story
Of being kidnapped by pirates on Lake Michigan
And kept in chains so he could not write me.
I pretended to believe it, though I knew very well
What he was doing, and that he met
The milliner, Mrs. Williams, now and then
When she went to the city to buy goods, as she
     said.
But a promise is a promise
And marriage is marriage,
And out of respect for my own character
I refused to be drawn into a divorce
By the scheme of a husband who had merely
     grown tired
Of his marital vow and duty.

JOSIAH TOMPKINS

I was well known and much beloved
And rich, as fortunes are reckoned
In Spoon River, where I had lived and worked.
That was the home for me,
Though all my children had flown afar—
Which is the way of Nature—all but one.
The boy, who was the baby, stayed at home,
To be my help in my failing years
And the solace of his mother.
But I grew weaker, as he grew stronger,
And he quarreled with me about the business,
And his wife said I was a hindrance to it;
And he won his mother to see as he did,
Till they tore me up to be transplanted
With them to her girlhood home in Missouri.
And so much of my fortune was gone at last,
Though I made the will just as he drew it,
He profited little by it.

MRS. KESSLER

Mr. Kessler, you know, was in the army,
And he drew six dollars a month as a pension,
And stood on the corner talking politics,
Or sat at home reading Grant's Memoirs;
And I supported the family by washing,
Learning the secrets of all the people
From their curtains, counterpanes, shirts and
    skirts.
For things that are new grow old at length,
They're replaced with better or none at all:
People are prospering or falling back.
And rents and patches widen with time;
No thread or needle can pace decay,
And there are stains that baffle soap,
And there are colors that run in spite of you,
Blamed though you are for spoiling a dress.
Handkerchiefs, napery, have their secrets—
The laundress, Life, knows all about it.
And I, who went to all the funerals
Held in Spoon River, swear I never
Saw a dead face without thinking it looked
Like something washed and ironed.

HARMON WHITNEY

Out of the lights and roar of cities,
Drifting down like a spark in Spoon River,
Burnt out with the fire of drink, and broken,
The paramour of a woman I took in self-contempt,
But to hide a wounded pride as well.
To be judged and loathed by a village of little
        minds—
I, gifted with tongues and wisdom,
Sunk here to the dust of the justice court,
A picker of rags in the rubbage of spites and
        wrongs,—
I, whom fortune smiled on! I in a village,
Spouting to gaping yokels pages of verse,
Out of the lore of golden years,
Or raising a laugh with a flash of filthy wit
When they bought the drinks to kindle my
        dying mind.
To be judged by you,
The soul of me hidden from you,
With its wound gangrened
By love for a wife who made the wound,
With her cold white bosom, treasonous, pure
        and hard,
Relentless to the last, when the touch of her hand,
At any time, might have cured me of the typhus,
Caught in the jungle of life where many are lost.
And only to think that my soul could not re-act,
Like Byron's did, in song, in something noble,
But turned on itself like a tortured snake—
Judge me this way, O world!

BERT KESSLER

I winged my bird,
Though he flew toward the setting sun;
But just as the shot rang out, he soared
Up and up through the splinters of golden light,
Till he turned right over, feathers ruffled,
With some of the down of him floating near,
And fell like a plummet into the grass.
I tramped about, parting the tangles,
Till I saw a splash of blood on a stump,
And the quail lying close to the rotten roots.
I reached my hand, but saw no brier,
But something pricked and stung and numbed it.
And then, in a second, I spied the rattler—
The shutters wide in his yellow eyes,
The head of him arched, sunk back in the rings
    of him,
A circle of filth, the color of ashes,
Or oak leaves bleached under layers of leaves.
I stood like a stone as he shrank and uncoiled
And started to crawl beneath the stump,
When I fell limp in the grass.

LAMBERT HUTCHINS

I have two monuments besides this granite
    obelisk:
One, the house I built on the hill,
With its spires, bay windows, and roof of slate;
The other, the lake-front in Chicago,
Where the railroad keeps a switching yard,
With whistling engines and crunching wheels,
And smoke and soot thrown over the city,
And the crash of cars along the boulevard,—
A blot like a hog-pen on the harbor
Of a great metropolis, foul as a sty.
I helped to give this heritage
To generations yet unborn, with my vote
In the House of Representatives,
And the lure of the thing was to be at rest
From the never-ending fright of need,
And to give my daughters gentle breeding,
And a sense of security in life.
But, you see, though I had the mansion house
And traveling passes and local distinction,
I could hear the whispers, whispers, whispers,
Wherever I went, and my daughters grew up
With a look as if someone were about to strike
    them;
And they married madly, helter-skelter,
Just to get out and have a change.
And what was the whole of the business worth?
Why, it wasn't worth a damn!

LILLIAN STEWART

I was the daughter of Lambert Hutchins,
Born in a cottage near the grist-mill,
Reared in the mansion there on the hill,
With its spires, bay windows, and roof of slate.
How proud my mother was of the mansion!
How proud of father's rise in the world!
And how my father loved and watched us,
And guarded our happiness.
But I believe the house was a curse,
For Father's fortune was little beside it;
And when my husband found he had married
A girl who was really poor,
He taunted me with the spires,
And called the house a fraud on the world,
A treacherous lure to young men, raising hopes
Of a dowry not to be had;
And a man while selling his vote
Should get enough from the people's betrayal
To wall the whole of his family in.
He vexed my life till I went back home
And lived like an old maid till I died,
Keeping house for Father.

HORTENSE ROBBINS

My name used to be in the papers daily
As having dined somewhere,
Or traveled somewhere,
Or rented a house in Paris,
Where I entertained the nobility.
I was forever eating or traveling,
Or taking the cure at Baden-Baden.
Now I am here to do honor
To Spoon River, here beside the family whence
　　I sprang.
No one cares now where I dined,
Or lived, or whom I entertained,
Or how often I took the cure at Baden-Baden!

BATTERTON DOBYNS

Did my widow flit about
From Mackinac to Los Angeles,
Resting and bathing and sitting an hour
Or more at the table over soup and meats
And delicate sweets and coffee?
I was cut down in my prime
From overwork and anxiety.
But I thought all along, whatever happens
I've kept my insurance up,
And there's something in the bank,
And a section of land in Manitoba.
But just as I slipped I had a vision
In a last delirium:
I saw myself lying nailed in a box
With a white lawn tie and a boutonnière,
And my wife was sitting by a window
Some place afar overlooking the sea;
She seemed so rested, ruddy and fat,
Although her hair was white.
And she smiled and said to a colored waiter:
"Another slice of roast beef, George.
Here's a nickel for your trouble."

JACOB GODBEY

How did you feel, you libertarians,
Who spent your talents rallying noble reasons
Around the saloon, as if Liberty
Was not to be found anywhere except at the bar
Or at a table, guzzling?
How did you feel, Ben Pantier, and the rest of you,
Who almost stoned me for a tyrant,
Garbed as a moralist,
And as a wry-faced ascetic frowning upon York-
     shire pudding,
Roast beef and ale and good will and rosy cheer—
Things you never saw in a grog-shop in your life?
How did you feel after I was dead and gone,
And your goddess, Liberty, unmasked as a
     strumpet,
Selling out the streets of Spoon River
To the insolent giants
Who manned the saloons from afar?
Did it occur to you that personal liberty
Is liberty of the mind,
Rather than of the belly?

WALTER SIMMONS

My parents thought that I would be
As great as Edison or greater:
For as a boy I made balloons
And wondrous kites and toys with clocks
And little engines with tracks to run on
And telephones of cans and thread.
I played the cornet and painted pictures,
Modeled in clay and took the part
Of the villain in the "Octoroon."*
But then at twenty-one I married
And had to live, and so, to live
I learned the trade of making watches
And kept the jewelry store on the square,
Thinking, thinking, thinking, thinking,—
Not of business, but of the engine
I studied the calculus to build.
And all Spoon River watched and waited
To see it work, but it never worked.
And a few kind souls believed my genius
Was somehow hampered by the store.
It wasn't true. The truth was this:
I didn't have the brains.

*"**Octoroon**" *The Octoroon* (1859) by Dion Boucicault, a melodrama
about slavery

TOM BEATTY

I was a lawyer like Harmon Whitney
Or Kinsey Keene or Garrison Standard,
For I tried the rights of property,
Although by lamp-light, for thirty years,
In that poker room in the opera house.
And I say to you that Life's a gambler
Head and shoulders above us all.
No mayor alive can close the house.
And if you lose, you can squeal as you will;
You'll not get back your money.
He makes the percentage hard to conquer;
He stacks the cards to catch your weakness
And not to meet your strength.
And he gives you seventy years to play:
For if you cannot win in seventy
You cannot win at all.
So, if you lose, get out of the room—
Get out of the room when your time is up.
It's mean to sit and fumble the cards,
And curse your losses, leaden-eyed,
Whining to try and try.

ROY BUTLER

If the learned Supreme Court of Illinois
Got at the secret of every case
As well as it does a case of rape
It would be the greatest court in the world.
A jury, of neighbors mostly, with "Butch" Weldy
As foreman, found me guilty in ten minutes
And two ballots on a case like this:
Richard Bandle and I had trouble over a fence,
And my wife and Mrs. Bandle quarreled
As to whether Ipava was a finer town than
    Table Grove.
I awoke one morning with the love of God
Brimming over my heart, so I went to see Richard
To settle the fence in the spirit of Jesus Christ.
I knocked on the door, and his wife opened;
She smiled and asked me in; I entered—
She slammed the door and began to scream,
"Take your hands off, you low down varlet!"
Just then her husband entered.
I waved my hands, choked up with words.
He went for his gun, and I ran out.
But neither the Supreme Court nor my wife
Believed a word she said.

SEARCY FOOTE

I wanted to go away to college
But rich Aunt Persis wouldn't help me.
So I made gardens and raked the lawns
And bought John Alden's books with my earnings
And toiled for the very means of life.
I wanted to marry Delia Prickett,
But how could I do it with what I earned?
And there was Aunt Persis more than seventy,
Who sat in a wheel-chair half alive,
With her throat so paralyzed, when she swallowed
The soup ran out of her mouth like a duck—
A gourmand yet, investing her income
In mortgages, fretting all the time
About her notes and rents and papers.
That day I was sawing wood for her,
And reading Proudhon in between.
I went in the house for a drink of water,
And there she sat asleep in her chair,
And Proudhon lying on the table,
And a bottle of chloroform on the book,
She used sometimes for an aching tooth!
I poured the chloroform on a handkerchief
And held it to her nose till she died.—
Oh Delia, Delia, you and Proudhon*
Steadied my hand, and the coroner
Said she died of heart failure.
I married Delia and got the money—
A joke on you, Spoon River?

*Proudhon Pierre-Joseph Proudhon (1809–1865), French reformer
and social theorist, most famous for his treatise on property com-
mencing with the assertion that "Property is theft," probably of
ironic relevance here

EDMUND POLLARD

I would I had thrust my hands of flesh
Into the disk-flowers bee-infested,
Into the mirror-like core of fire
Of the light of life, the sun of delight.
For what are anthers worth or petals
Or halo-rays? Mockeries, shadows
Of the heart of the flower, the central flame!
All is yours, young passer-by;
Enter the banquet room with the thought;
Don't sidle in as if you were doubtful
Whether you're welcome—the feast is yours!
Nor take but a little, refusing more
With a bashful "Thank you," when you're hungry.
Is your soul alive? Then let it feed!
Leave no balconies where you can climb;
Nor milk-white bosoms where you can rest;
Nor golden heads with pillows to share;
Nor wine cups while the wine is sweet;
Nor ecstasies of body or soul,
You will die, no doubt, but die while living
In depths of azure, rapt and mated,
Kissing the queen-bee, Life!

THOMAS TREVELYAN

Reading in Ovid the sorrowful story of Itys,
Son of the love of Tereus and Procne, slain
For the guilty passion of Tereus for Philomela,
The flesh of him served to Tereus by Procne,
And the wrath of Tereus, the murderess pursuing
Till the gods made Philomela a nightingale,
Lute of the rising moon, and Procne a swallow!
Oh livers and artists of Hellas centuries gone,
Sealing in little thuribles dreams and wisdom,
Incense beyond all price, forever fragrant,
A breath whereof makes clear the eyes of the soul!
How I inhaled its sweetness here in Spoon River!
The thurible* opening when I had lived and
    learned
How all of us kill the children of love, and all
    of us,
Knowing not what we do, devour their flesh;
And all of us change to singers, although it be
But once in our lives, or change—alas!—to
    swallows,
To twitter amid cold winds and falling leaves!

*__thurible__ a censer, vessel for burning incense

PERCIVAL SHARP

Observe the clasped hands!*
Are they hands of farewell or greeting,
Hands that I helped or hands that helped me?
Would it not be well to carve a hand
With an inverted thumb, like Elagabalus?†
And yonder is a broken chain,‡
The weakest-link idea perhaps—
But what was it?
And lambs, some lying down,
Others standing, as if listening to the shepherd—
Others bearing a cross, one foot lifted up—
Why not chisel a few shambles?§
And fallen columns! Carve the pedestal, please,
Or the foundations; let us see the cause of the fall.
And compasses and mathematical instruments,
In irony of the under tenants' ignorance
Of determinants and the calculus of variations.
And anchors, for those who never sailed.
And gates ajar—yes, so they were;
You left them open and stray goats entered your
    garden.
And an eye watching like one of the Arimaspi—**
So did you—with one eye.
And angels blowing trumpets—you are
    heralded—

*clasped hands usually an emblem of friendship, frequently used,
like the ‡broken chain, on American tombstones
†Elagabalus or Heliogabalus: Varius Avitus Bassanius (205–222),
unspeakably depraved and brutal Roman emperor; the inverted
thumb would signal the death of a gladiator in the arena
§shambles a slaughterhouse
**Arimaspi mythical one-eyed people of Syria, constantly warring
with the Griffins

It is your horn and your angel and your family's
   estimate.
It is all very well, but for myself I know
I stirred certain vibrations in Spoon River
Which are my true epitaph, more lasting than
   stone.

HIRAM SCATES

I tried to win the nomination
For president of the County-board
And I made speeches all over the County
Denouncing Solomon Purple, my rival,
As an enemy of the people,
In league with the master-foes of man.
Young idealists, broken warriors,
Hobbling on one crutch of hope,
Souls that stake their all on the truth,
Losers of worlds at heaven's bidding,
Flocked about me and followed my voice
As the savior of the County.
But Solomon won the nomination;
And then I faced about,
And rallied my followers to his standard,
And made him victor, made him King
Of the Golden Mountain* with the door
Which closed on my heels just as I entered,
Flattered by Solomon's invitation,
To be the County-board's secretary.
And out in the cold stood all my followers:
Young idealists, broken warriors
Hobbling on one crutch of hope—
Souls that staked their all on the truth,
Losers of worlds at heaven's bidding,
Watching the Devil kick the Millennium
Over the Golden Mountain.

---

*King of the Golden Mountain in one of Grimm's Fairy Tales,
a wandering youth who withstands enchantments to accede to
a kingdom

PELEG POAGUE

Horses and men are just alike.
There was my stallion, Billy Lee,
Black as a cat and trim as a deer,
With an eye of fire, keen to start,
And he could hit the fastest speed
Of any racer around Spoon River.
But just as you'd think he couldn't lose,
With his lead of fifty yards or more,
He'd rear himself and throw the rider,
And fall back over, tangled up,
Completely gone to pieces.
You see he was a perfect fraud:
He couldn't win, he couldn't work,
He was too light to haul or plow with,
And no one wanted colts from him.
And when I tried to drive him—well,
He ran away and killed me.

JEDUTHAN HAWLEY

There would be a knock at the door
And I would arise at midnight and go to the shop,
Where belated travelers would hear me
    hammering
Sepulchral boards and tacking satin.
And often I wondered who would go with me
To the distant land, our names the theme
For talk, in the same week, for I've observed
Two always go together.
Chase Henry was paired with Edith Conant;
And Jonathan Somers with Willie Metcalf;
And Editor Hamblin with Francis Turner,
When he prayed to live longer than Editor
    Whedon;
And Thomas Rhodes with widow McFarlane;
And Emily Sparks with Barry Holden;
And Oscar Hummel with Davis Matlock;
And Editor Whedon with Fiddler Jones;
And Faith Matheny with Dorcas Gustine.
And I, the solemnest man in town,
Stepped off with Daisy Fraser.

ABEL MELVENY

I bought every kind of machine that's known—
Grinders, shellers, planters, mowers,
Mills and rakes and ploughs and threshers—
And all of them stood in the rain and sun,
Getting rusted, warped and battered,
For I had no sheds to store them in,
And no use for most of them.
And toward the last, when I thought it over,
There by my window, growing clearer
About myself, as my pulse slowed down,
And looked at one of the mills I bought—
Which I didn't have the slightest need of,
As things turned out, and I never ran—
A fine machine, once brightly varnished,
And eager to do its work,
Now with its paint washed off—
I saw myself as a good machine
That Life had never used.

OAKS TUTT

My mother was for woman's rights
And my father was the rich miller at London
      Mills.
I dreamed of the wrongs of the world and wanted
      to right them.
When my father died, I set out to see peoples
      and countries
In order to learn how to reform the world.
I traveled through many lands.
I saw the ruins of Rome,
And the ruins of Athens,
And the ruins of Thebes.
And I sat by moonlight amid the necropolis of
      Memphis.
There I was caught up by wings of flame,
And a voice from heaven said to me:
"Injustice, Untruth destroyed them. Go forth!
Preach Justice! Preach Truth!"
And I hastened back to Spoon River
To say farewell to my mother before beginning
      my work.
They all saw a strange light in my eye.
And by and by, when I talked, they discovered
What had come in my mind.
Then Jonathan Swift Somers challenged me to
      debate
The subject, (I taking the negative):
"Pontius Pilate, the Greatest Philosopher of the
      World."
And he won the debate by saying at last,
"Before you reform the world, Mr. Tutt,
Please answer the question of Pontius Pilate:
'What is Truth?'"

ELLIOTT HAWKINS

I looked like Abraham Lincoln.
I was one of you, Spoon River, in all fellowship,
But standing for the rights of property and for
    order.
A regular church attendant,
Sometimes appearing in your town meetings to
    warn you
Against the evils of discontent and envy,
And to denounce those who tried to destroy the
    Union,*
And to point to the peril of the Knights of Labor.†
My success and my example are inevitable
    influences
In your young men and in generations to come,
In spite of attacks of newspapers like the *Clarion*;
A regular visitor at Springfield,
When the Legislature was in session,
To prevent raids upon the railroads,
And the men building up the state.
Trusted by them and by you, Spoon River, equally
In spite of the whispers that I was a lobbyist.
Moving quietly through the world, rich and
    courted.
Dying at last, of course, but lying here
Under a stone with an open book carved upon it
And the words *"Of such is the Kingdom of
    Heaven."*‡

---

*Union** in the Civil War, not to be confused with the reference,
in the next line, to the early fraternal labor union, †**the Knights
of Labor**
‡**"Of such is the Kingdom of Heaven"** the formula is from
Mark 10:14

And now, you world-savers, who reaped nothing
    in life,
And in death have neither stones nor epitaphs,
How do you like your silence from mouths
    stopped
With the dust of my triumphant career?

VOLTAIRE JOHNSON

Why did you bruise me with your rough places
If you did not want me to tell you about them?
And stifle me with your stupidities,
If you did not want me to expose them?
And nail me with the nails of cruelty,
If you did not want me to pluck the nails forth
And fling them in your faces?
And starve me because I refused to obey you,
If you did not want me to undermine your
     tyranny?
I might have been as soul serene
As William Wordsworth except for you!
But what a coward you are, Spoon River,
When you drove me to stand in a magic circle
By the sword of Truth described!
And then to whine and curse your burns,
And curse my power who stood and laughed
Amid ironical lightning!

ENGLISH THORNTON

Here! You sons of the men
Who fought with Washington at Valley Forge,
And whipped Black Hawk at Starved Rock,
Arise! Do battle with the descendants of those
Who bought land in the loop* when it was
        waste sand,
And sold blankets and guns to the army of Grant,
And sat in legislatures in the early days,
Taking bribes from the railroads!
Arise! Do battle with the fops and bluffs,
The pretenders and figurantes of the society
        column,
And the yokel souls whose daughters marry
        counts;
And the parasites on great ideas,
And the noisy riders of great causes,
And the heirs of ancient thefts.
Arise! And make the city yours,
And the State yours—
You who are sons of the hardy yeomanry of the
        forties!
By God! If you do not destroy these vermin
My avenging ghost will wipe out
Your city and your state.

*loop the "Loop" of central downtown Chicago

ENOCH DUNLAP

How many times, during the twenty years
I was your leader, friends of Spoon River,
Did you neglect the convention and caucus,
And leave the burden on my hands
Of guarding and saving the people's cause?—
Sometimes because you were ill;
Or your grandmother was ill;
Or you drank too much and fell asleep;
Or else you said: "He is our leader,
All will be well; he fights for us;
We have nothing to do but follow."
But oh, how you cursed me when I fell,
And cursed me, saying I had betrayed you,
In leaving the caucus room for a moment,
When the people's enemies, there assembled,
Waited and watched for a chance to destroy
The Sacred Rights of the People.
You common rabble! I left the caucus
To go to the urinal!

IDA FRICKEY

Nothing in life is alien to you:
I was a penniless girl from Summum
Who stepped from the morning train in Spoon
   River.
All the houses stood before me with closed doors
And drawn shades—I was barred out;
I had no place or part in any of them.
And I walked past the old McNeely mansion,
A castle of stone 'mid walks and gardens,
With workmen about the place on guard,
And the County and State upholding it
For its lordly owner, full of pride.
I was so hungry I had a vision:
I saw a giant pair of scissors
Dip from the sky, like the beam of a dredge,
And cut the house in two like a curtain.
But at the "Commercial" I saw a man,
Who winked at me as I asked for work—
It was Wash McNeely's son.
He proved the link in the chain of title
To half my ownership of the mansion,
Through a breach of promise suit—the scissors.
So, you see, the house, from the day I was born,
Was only waiting for me.

SETH COMPTON

When I died, the circulating library
Which I built up for Spoon River,
And managed for the good of inquiring minds,
Was sold at auction on the public square,
As if to destroy the last vestige
Of my memory and influence.
For those of you who could not see the virtue
Of knowing Volney's "Ruins"* as well as But-
    ler's "Analogy"†
And "Faust" as well as "Evangeline,"
Were really the power in the village,
And often you asked me,
"What is the use of knowing the evil in the
    world?"
I am out of your way now, Spoon River,
Choose your own good and call it good.
For I could never make you see
That no one knows what is good
Who knows not what is evil;
And no one knows what is true
Who knows not what is false.

*Volney's "Ruins" the Ruins, or Meditations on the Revolutions of Empires (1791) of Constantin François de Chasseboeuf, Comte de Volney (1757–1820), a generally libertarian and egalitarian writer
†Butler's "Analogy" Joseph Butler (1692–1752), author of the important Analogy of Religion, which sought to reconcile Natural and Revealed Religion and defend Christianity against Deism

FELIX SCHMIDT

It was only a little house of two rooms—
Almost like a child's play-house—
With scarce five acres of ground around it;
And I had so many children to feed
And school and clothe, and a wife who was sick
From bearing children.
One day lawyer Whitney came along
And proved to me that Christian Dallman,
Who owned three thousand acres of land,
Had bought the eighty that adjoined me
In eighteen hundred and seventy-one
For eleven dollars, at a sale for taxes,
While my father lay in his mortal illness.
So the quarrel arose and I went to law.
But when we came to the proof,
A survey of the land showed clear as day
That Dallman's tax deed covered my ground
And my little house of two rooms.
It served me right for stirring him up.
I lost my case and lost my place.
I left the court room and went to work
As Christian Dallman's tenant.

SCHRŒDER THE FISHERMAN

I sat on the bank above Bernadotte
And dropped crumbs in the water,
Just to see the minnows bump each other,
Until the strongest got the prize.
Or I went to my little pasture,
Where the peaceful swine were asleep in the
       wallow,
Or nosing each other lovingly,
And emptied a basket of yellow corn,
And watched them push and squeal and bite,
And trample each other to get the corn.
And I saw how Christian Dallman's farm,
Of more than three thousand acres,
Swallowed the patch of Felix Schmidt,
As a bass will swallow a minnow.
And I say if there's anything in man—
Spirit, or conscience, or breath of God
That makes him different from fishes or hogs,
I'd like to see it work!

RICHARD BONE

When I first came to Spoon River
I did not know whether what they told me
Was true or false.
They would bring me the epitaph
And stand around the shop while I worked
And say "He was so kind," "He was wonderful,"
"She was the sweetest woman," "He was a consis-
    tent Christian."
And I chiseled for them whatever they wished,
All in ignorance of its truth.
But later, as I lived among the people here,
I knew how near to the life
Were the epitaphs that were ordered for them as
    they died.
But still I chiseled whatever they paid me to chisel
And made myself party to the false chronicles
Of the stones,
Even as the historian does who writes
Without knowing the truth,
Or because he is influenced to hide it.

SILAS DEMENT

It was moon-light, and the earth sparkled
With new-fallen frost.
It was midnight and not a soul was abroad.
Out of the chimney of the court-house
A grey-hound of smoke leapt and chased
The northwest wind.
I carried a ladder to the landing of the stairs
And leaned it against the frame of the trap-door
In the ceiling of the portico,
And I crawled under the roof and amid the rafters
And flung among the seasoned timbers
A lighted handful of oil-soaked waste.
Then I came down and slunk away.
In a little while the fire-bell rang—
Clang! Clang! Clang!
And the Spoon River ladder company
Came with a dozen buckets and began to pour
    water
On the glorious bon-fire, growing hotter,
Higher and brighter, till the walls fell in,
And the limestone columns where Lincoln stood
Crashed like trees when the woodman fells
    them . . .
When I came back from Joliet*
There was a new court-house with a dome.
For I was punished like all who destroy
The past for the sake of the future.

*Joliet where there is an Illinois state prison

DILLARD SISSMAN

The buzzards wheel slowly
In wide circles, in a sky
Faintly hazed as from dust from the road.
And a wind sweeps through the pasture where
      I lie
Beating the grass into long waves.
My kite is above the wind,
Though now and then it wobbles,
Like a man shaking his shoulders;
And the tail streams out momentarily,
Then sinks to rest.
And the buzzards wheel and wheel,
Sweeping the zenith with wide circles
Above my kite. And the hills sleep.
And a farm house, white as snow,
Peeps from green trees—far away.
And I watch my kite,
For the thin moon will kindle herself ere long,
Then she will swing like a pendulum dial
To the tail of my kite.
A spurt of flame like a water-dragon
Dazzles my eyes—
I am shaken as a banner!

JONATHAN HOUGHTON

There is the caw of a crow,
And the hesitant song of a thrush.
There is the tinkle of a cowbell far away,
And the voice of a ploughman on Shipley's hill.
The forest beyond the orchard is still
With midsummer stillness;
And along the road a wagon chuckles,
Loaded with corn, going to Atterbury.
And an old man sits under a tree asleep,
And an old woman crosses the road,
Coming from the orchard with a bucket of
    blackberries.
And a boy lies in the grass
Near the feet of the old man,
And looks up at the sailing clouds,
And longs, and longs, and longs
For what, he knows not:
For manhood, for life, for the unknown world!
Then thirty years passed,
And the boy returned worn out by life
And found the orchard vanished,
And the forest gone,
And the house made over,
And the roadway filled with dust from
    automobiles—
And himself desiring The Hill!

E. C. CULBERTSON

Is it true, Spoon River,
That in the hall-way of the new court-house
There is a tablet of bronze
Containing the embossed faces
Of Editor Whedon and Thomas Rhodes?
And is it true that my successful labors
In the County Board, without which
Not one stone would have been placed on another,
And the contributions out of my own pocket
To build the temple, are but memories among
      the people,
Gradually fading away, and soon to descend
With them to this oblivion where I lie?
In truth, I can so believe.
For it is a law of the Kingdom of Heaven
That whoso enters the vineyard at the eleventh
      hour
Shall receive a full day's pay.
And it is a law of the Kingdom of this World
That those who first oppose a good work
Seize it and make it their own,
When the corner-stone is laid,
And memorial tablets are erected.

SHACK DYE

The white men played all sorts of jokes on me.
They took big fish off my hook
And put little ones on, while I was away
Getting a stringer, and made me believe
I hadn't seen aright the fish I had caught.
When Burr Robbins circus came to town
They got the ring master to let a tame leopard
Into the ring, and made me believe
I was whipping a wild beast like Samson
When I, for an offer of fifty dollars,
Dragged him out to his cage.
One time I entered my blacksmith shop
And shook as I saw some horse-shoes crawling
Across the floor, as if alive—
Walter Simmons had put a magnet
Under the barrel of water.
Yet everyone of you, you white men,
Was fooled about fish and about leopards too,
And you didn't know any more than the horse-
    shoes did
What moved you about Spoon River.

HILDRUP TUBBS

I made two fights for the people.
First I left my party, bearing the gonfalon*
Of independence, for reform, and was defeated.
Next I used my rebel strength
To capture the standard of my old party—
And I captured it, but I was defeated.
Discredited and discarded, misanthropical,
I turned to the solace of gold
And I used my remnant of power
To fasten myself like a saprophyte
Upon the putrescent carcass
Of Thomas Rhodes' bankrupt bank,
As assignee of the fund.
Everyone now turned from me.
My hair grew white,
My purple lusts grew gray,
Tobacco and whiskey lost their savor
And for years Death ignored me
As he does a hog.

*gonfalon banner

HENRY TRIPP

The bank broke and I lost my savings.
I was sick of the tiresome game in Spoon River
And I made up my mind to run away
And leave my place in life and my family;
But just as the midnight train pulled in,
Quick off the steps jumped Cully Green
And Martin Vise, and began to fight
To settle their ancient rivalry,
Striking each other with fists that sounded
Like the blows of knotted clubs.
Now it seemed to me that Cully was winning,
When his bloody face broke into a grin
Of sickly cowardice, leaning on Martin
And whining out "We're good friends, Mart,
You know that I'm your friend."
But a terrible punch from Martin knocked him
Around and around and into a heap.
And then they arrested me as a witness,
And I lost my train and staid in Spoon River
To wage my battle of life to the end.
Oh, Cully Green, you were my savior—
You, so ashamed and drooped for years,
Loitering listless about the streets,
And tying rags 'round your festering soul,
Who failed to fight it out.

GRANVILLE CALHOUN

I wanted to be County Judge
One more term, so as to round out a service
Of thirty years.
But my friends left me and joined my enemies,
And they elected a new man.
Then a spirit of revenge seized me,
And I infected my four sons with it,
And I brooded upon retaliation,
Until the great physician, Nature,
Smote me through with paralysis
To give my soul and body a rest.
Did my sons get power and money?
Did they serve the people or yoke them,
To till and harvest fields of self?
For how could they ever forget
My face at my bed-room window,
Sitting helpless amid my golden cages
Of singing canaries,
Looking at the old court-house?

HENRY C. CALHOUN

I reached the highest place in Spoon River,
But through what bitterness of spirit!
The face of my father, sitting speechless,
Child-like, watching his canaries,
And looking at the court-house window
Of the county judge's room,
And his admonitions to me to seek
My own in life, and punish Spoon River
To avenge the wrong the people did him,
Filled me with furious energy
To seek for wealth and seek for power.
But what did he do but send me along
The path that leads to the grove of the Furies?
I followed the path and I tell you this:
On the way to the grove you'll pass the Fates,
Shadow-eyed, bent over their weaving.
Stop for a moment, and if you see
The thread of revenge leap out of the shuttle
Then quickly snatch from Atropos*
The shears and cut it, lest your sons,
And the children of them and their children
Wear the envenomed robe.

Atropos of the three Fates of classical mythology, Atropos was
the one who cut the thread of life which the other two spun and
measured (Clotho and Lachesis)

ALFRED MOIR

Why was I not devoured by self-contempt,
And rotted down by indifference
And impotent revolt like "Indignation" Jones?
Why, with all of my errant steps,
Did I miss the fate of Willard Fluke?
And why, though I stood at Burchard's bar,
As a sort of decoy for the house to the boys
To buy the drinks, did the curse of drink
Fall on me like rain that runs off,
Leaving the soul of me dry and clean?
And why did I never kill a man
Like Jack McGuire?
But instead I mounted a little in life,
And I owe it all to a book I read.
But why did I go to Mason City,
Where I chanced to see the book in a window,
With its garish cover luring my eye?
And why did my soul respond to the book,*
As I read it over and over?

*the book we may guess that it was a copy of Shelley's poems; the
description recalls Masters' own reminiscence of "a book bound in
red, with golden scrolls and decorations" that he saw in a shop
window as a boy and which he immediately bought and read

PERRY ZOLL

My thanks, friends of the County Scientific
    Association,
For this modest boulder,
And its little tablet of bronze.
Twice I tried to join your honored body,
And was rejected,
And when my little brochure
On the intelligence of plants
Began to attract attention
You almost voted me in.
After that I grew beyond the need of you
And your recognition.
Yet I do not reject your memorial stone,
Seeing that I should, in so doing,
Deprive you of honor to yourselves.

DIPPOLD THE OPTICIAN

What do you see now?
Globes of red, yellow, purple.
Just a moment! And now?
My father and mother and sisters.
Yes! And now?
Knights at arms, beautiful women, kind faces.
Try this.
A field of grain—a city.
Very good! And now?
A young woman with angels bending over her.
A heavier lens! And now?
Many women with bright eyes and open lips.
Try this.
Just a goblet on a table.
Oh I see! Try this lens!
Just an open space—I see nothing in particular.
Well, now!
Pine trees, a lake, a summer sky.
That's better. And now?
A book.
Read a page for me.
I can't. My eyes are carried beyond the page.
Try this lens.
Depths of air.
Excellent! And now?
Light, just light, making everything below it a
     toy world.
Very well, we'll make the glasses accordingly.

MAGRADY GRAHAM

Tell me, was Altgeld* elected Governor?
For when the returns began to come in
And Cleveland was sweeping the East,
It was too much for you, poor old heart,
Who had striven for democracy
In the long, long years of defeat.
And like a watch that is worn
I felt you growing slower until you stopped.
Tell me, was Altgeld elected,
And what did he do?
Did they bring his head on a platter to a dancer,
Or did he triumph for the people?
For when I saw him
And took his hand,
The child-like blueness of his eyes
Moved me to tears,
And there was an air of eternity about him,
Like the cold, clear light that rests at dawn
On the hills!

*Altgeld see note for Adam Weirauch, p. 126

ARCHIBALD HIGBIE

I loathed you, Spoon River. I tried to rise above
    you,
I was ashamed of you. I despised you
As the place of my nativity.
And there in Rome, among the artists,
Speaking Italian, speaking French,
I seemed to myself at times to be free
Of every trace of my origin.
I seemed to be reaching the heights of art
And to breathe the air that the masters breathed,
And to see the world with their eyes.
But still they'd pass my work and say:
"What are you driving at, my friend?
Sometimes the face looks like Apollo's,
At others it has a trace of Lincoln's."
There was no culture, you know, in Spoon River,
And I burned with shame and held my peace.
And what could I do, all covered over
And weighted down with western soil,
Except aspire, and pray for another
Birth in the world, with all of Spoon River
Rooted out of my soul?

TOM MERRITT

At first I suspected something—
She acted so calm and absent-minded.
And one day I heard the back door shut,
As I entered the front, and I saw him slink
Back of the smokehouse into the lot,
And run across the field.
And I meant to kill him on sight.
But that day, walking near Fourth Bridge,
Without a stick or a stone at hand,
All of a sudden I saw him standing,
Scared to death, holding his rabbits,
And all I could say was, "Don't, Don't, Don'
As he aimed and fired at my heart.

MRS. MERRITT

Silent before the jury,
Returning no word to the judge when he asked me
If I had aught to say against the sentence,
Only shaking my head.
What could I say to people who thought
That a woman of thirty-five was at fault
When her lover of nineteen killed her husband?
Even though she had said to him over and over,
"Go away, Elmer, go far away,
I have maddened your brain with the gift of my
    body:
You will do some terrible thing."
And just as I feared, he killed my husband;
With which I had nothing to do, before God!
Silent for thirty years in prison!
And the iron gates of Joliet*
Swung as the gray and silent trusties
Carried me out in a coffin.

---

*iron gates of Joliet** the Illinois State Prison is in Joliet; the "iron
gates of life" in Andrew Marvell's "To His Coy Mistress" are
ironically invoked here; the word "trusties" is resonantly used

ELMER KARR

What but the love of God could have softened
And made forgiving the people of Spoon River
Toward me who wronged the bed of Thomas
        Merritt
And murdered him beside?
Oh, loving hearts that took me in again
When I returned from fourteen years in prison!
Oh, helping hands that in the church received me,
And heard with tears my penitent confession,
Who took the sacrament of bread and wine!
Repent, ye living ones, and rest with Jesus.

ELIZABETH CHILDERS

Dust of my dust,
And dust with my dust,
O, child who died as you entered the world,
Dead with my death!
Not knowing Breath, though you tried so hard,
With a heart that beat when you lived with me,
And stopped when you left me for Life.
It is well, my child. For you never traveled
The long, long way that begins with school days,
When little fingers blur under the tears
That fall on the crooked letters.
And the earliest wound, when a little mate
Leaves you alone for another;
And sickness, and the face of Fear by the bed;
The death of a father or mother;
Or shame for them, or poverty;
The maiden sorrow of school days ended;
And eyeless Nature that makes you drink
From the cup of Love, though you know it's
      poisoned;
To whom would your flower-face have been
      lifted?
Botanist, weakling? Cry of what blood to yours?—
Pure or foul, for it makes no matter,
It's blood that calls to our blood.
And then your children—oh, what might they be?
And what your sorrow? Child! Child!
Death is better than Life!

EDITH CONANT

We stand about this place—we, the memories;
And shade our eyes because we dread to read:
"June 17th, 1884, aged 21 years and 3 days."
And all things are changed.
And we—we, the memories, stand here for our-
        selves alone,
For no eye marks us, or would know why we
        are here.
Your husband is dead, your sister lives far away,
Your father is bent with age;
He has forgotten you, he scarcely leaves the house
Any more.
No one remembers your exquisite face,
Your lyric voice!
How you sang, even on the morning you were
        stricken,
With piercing sweetness, with thrilling sorrow,
Before the advent of the child which died with
        you.
It is all forgotten, save by us, the memories,
Who are forgotten by the world.
All is changed, save the river and the hill—
Even they are changed.
Only the burning sun and the quiet stars are the
        same.
And we—we, the memories, stand here in awe,
Our eyes closed with the weariness of tears—
In immeasurable weariness!

CHARLES WEBSTER

The pine woods on the hill,
And the farmhouse miles away,
Showed clear as though behind a lens
Under a sky of peacock blue!
But a blanket of cloud by afternoon
Muffled the earth. And you walked the road
And the clover field, where the only sound
Was the cricket's liquid tremolo.
Then the sun went down between great drifts
Of distant storms. For a rising wind
Swept clean the sky and blew the flames
Of the unprotected stars;
And swayed the russet moon,
Hanging between the rim of the hill
And the twinkling boughs of the apple orchard.
You walked the shore in thought
Where the throats of the waves were like whip-
    poor-wills
Singing beneath the water and crying
To the wash of the wind in the cedar trees,
Till you stood, too full for tears, by the cot,
And looking up saw Jupiter,
Tipping the spire of the giant pine,
And looking down saw my vacant chair,
Rocked by the wind on the lonely porch—
Be brave, Beloved!

FATHER MALLOY

You are over there, Father Malloy,
Where holy ground is, and the cross marks
      every grave,
Not here with us on the hill—
Us of wavering faith, and clouded vision
And drifting hope, and unforgiven sins.
You were so human, Father Malloy,
Taking a friendly glass sometimes with us,
Siding with us who would rescue Spoon River
From the coldness and the dreariness of village
      morality.
You were like a traveler who brings a little box
      of sand
From the wastes about the pyramids
And makes them real and Egypt real.
You were a part of and related to a great past,
And yet you were so close to many of us.
You believed in the joy of life.
You did not seem to be ashamed of the flesh.
You faced life as it is,
And as it changes.
Some of us almost came to you, Father Malloy,
Seeing how your church had divined the heart,
And provided for it,
Through Peter the Flame,
Peter the Rock.*

---

*Peter . . . Rock St. Peter, invoked as "the rock" upon which Christ
would build his church in *Matthew* 16:18, and probably as one of
the "ministers" made into a flame in *Hebrews* 1:7

AMI GREEN

Not "a youth with hoary head and haggard eye,"
But an old man with a smooth skin
And black hair!
I had the face of a boy as long as I lived,
And for years a soul that was stiff and bent,
In a world which saw me just as a jest,
To be hailed familiarly when it chose,
And loaded up as a man when it chose,
Being neither man nor boy.
In truth it was soul as well as body
Which never matured, and I say to you
That the much-sought prize of eternal youth
Is just arrested growth.

CALVIN CAMPBELL

Ye who are kicking against Fate,
Tell me how it is that on this hill-side,
Running down to the river,
Which fronts the sun and the south-wind,
This plant draws from the air and soil
Poison and becomes poison ivy?
And this plant draws from the same air and soil
Sweet elixirs and colors and becomes arbutus?
And both flourish?
You may blame Spoon River for what it is,
But whom do you blame for the will in you
That feeds itself and makes you dock-weed,
Jimpson, dandelion or mullen
And which can never use any soil or air
So as to make you jessamine or wistaria?

HENRY LAYTON

Whoever thou art who passest by
Know that my father was gentle,
And my mother was violent,
While I was born the whole of such hostile halves,
Not intermixed and fused,
But each distinct, feebly soldered together.
Some of you saw me as gentle,
Some as violent,
Some as both.
But neither half of me wrought my ruin.
It was the falling asunder of halves,
Never a part of each other,
That left me a lifeless soul.

HARLAN SEWALL

You never understood, O unknown one,
Why it was I repaid
Your devoted friendship and delicate ministrations
First with diminished thanks,
Afterward by gradually withdrawing my presence
    from you,
So that I might not be compelled to thank you,
And then with silence which followed upon
Our final Separation.
You had cured my diseased soul. But to cure it
You saw my disease, you knew my secret,
And that is why I fled from you.
For though when our bodies rise from pain
We kiss forever the watchful hands
That gave us wormwood, while we shudder
For thinking of the wormwood,
A soul that's cured is a different matter,
For there we'd blot from memory
The soft-toned words, the searching eyes,
And stand forever oblivious,
Not so much of the sorrow itself
As of the hand that healed it.

IPPOLIT KONOVALOFF

I was a gun-smith in Odessa.
One night the police broke in the room
Where a group of us were reading Spencer.*
And seized our books and arrested us.
But I escaped and came to New York
And thence to Chicago, and then to Spoon River,
Where I could study my Kant in peace
And eke out a living repairing guns!
Look at my moulds! My architectonics!
One for a barrel, one for a hammer,
And others for other parts of a gun!
Well, now suppose no gun-smith living
Had anything else but duplicate moulds
Of these I show you—well, all guns
Would be just alike, with a hammer to hit
The cap and a barrel to carry the shot,
All acting alike for themselves, and all
Acting against each other alike.
And there would be your world of guns!
Which nothing could ever free from itself
Except a Moulder with different moulds
To mould the metal over.

*Spencer Herbert Spencer (1820–1903), evolutionary, scientistic
philosopher

HENRY PHIPPS

I was the Sunday school superintendent,
The dummy president of the wagon works
And the canning factory,
Acting for Thomas Rhodes and the banking clique;
My son the cashier of the bank,
Wedded to Rhodes' daughter,
My week days spent in making money,
My Sundays at church and in prayer.
In everything a cog in the wheel of things-as-
        they-are:
Of money, master and man, made white
With the paint of the Christian creed.
And then:
The bank collapsed. I stood and looked at the
        wrecked machine—
The wheels with blow-holes stopped with putty
        and painted;
The rotten bolts, the broken rods;
And only the hopper for souls fit to be used again
In a new devourer of life, when newspapers,
        judges and money-magicians
Build over again.
I was stripped to the bone, but I lay in the Rock of
        Ages,
Seeing now through the game, no longer a dupe,
And knowing "the upright shall dwell in the land
But the years of the wicked shall be shortened."*
Then suddenly, Dr. Meyers discovered

*"the upright . . . shortened" a conflation of *Proverbs* 2:21 and
10:27

A cancer in my liver.
I was not, after all, the particular care of God!
Why, even thus standing on a peak
Above the mists through which I had climbed,
And ready for larger life in the world,
Eternal forces
Moved me on with a push.

HARRY WILMANS

I was just turned twenty-one,
And Henry Phipps, the Sunday school superintendent,
Made a speech in Bindle's Opera House.
"The honor of the flag must be upheld," he said,
"Whether it be assailed by a barbarous tribe of
      Tagalogs*
Or the greatest power in Europe."
And we cheered and cheered the speech and the
      flag he waved
As he spoke.
And I went to the war in spite of my father,
And followed the flag till I saw it raised
By our camp in a rice field near Manila,
And all of us cheered and cheered it.
But there were flies and poisonous things;
And there was the deadly water,
And the cruel heat,
And the sickening, putrid food;
And the smell of the trench just back of the tents
Where the soldiers went to empty themselves;
And there were the whores who followed us, full
      of syphilis;
And beastly acts between ourselves or alone,
With bullying, hatred, degradation among us,
And days of loathing and nights of fear
To the hour of the charge through the steaming
      swamp,
Following the flag,
Till I fell with a scream, shot through the guts.
Now there's a flag over me in Spoon River!
A flag! A flag!

*Tagalogs people native to the Philippines

JOHN WASSON

Oh! the dew-wet grass of the meadow in North
    Carolina
Through which Rebecca followed me wailing,
    wailing,
One child in her arms, and three that ran along
    wailing,
Lengthening out the farewell to me off to the war
    with the British,
And then the long, hard years down to the day
    of Yorktown.
And then my search for Rebecca,
Finding her at last in Virginia,
Two children dead in the meanwhile.
We went by oxen to Tennessee,
Thence after years to Illinois,
At last to Spoon River.
We cut the buffalo grass,
We felled the forests,
We built the school houses, built the bridges,
Leveled the roads and tilled the fields
Alone with poverty, scourges, death—
If Harry Wilmans who fought the Filipinos
Is to have a flag on his grave
Take it from mine!

MANY SOLDIERS

The idea danced before us as a flag;
The sound of martial music;
The thrill of carrying a gun;
Advancement in the world on coming home;
A glint of glory, wrath for foes;
A dream of duty to country or to God.
But these were things in ourselves, shining be-
     fore us,
They were not the power behind us,
Which was the Almighty hand of Life,
Like fire at earth's center making mountains,
Or pent up waters that cut them through.
Do you remember the iron band
The blacksmith, Shack Dye, welded
Around the oak on Bennet's lawn,
From which to swing a hammock,
That daughter Janet might repose in, reading
On summer afternoons?
And that the growing tree at last
Sundered the iron band?
But not a cell in all the tree
Knew aught save that it thrilled with life,
Nor cared because the hammock fell
In the dust with Milton's Poems.

GODWIN JAMES

Harry Wilmans! You who fell in a swamp
Near Manila, following the flag,
You were not wounded by the greatness of a
    dream,
Or destroyed by ineffectual work,
Or driven to madness by Satanic snags;
You were not torn by aching nerves,
Nor did you carry great wounds to your old age.
You did not starve, for the government fed you.
You did not suffer yet cry "forward"
To an army which you led
Against a foe with mocking smiles,
Sharper than bayonets. You were not smitten
    down
By invisible bombs. You were not rejected
By those for whom you were defeated.
You did not eat the savorless bread
Which a poor alchemy had made from ideals.
You went to Manila, Harry Wilmans,
While I enlisted in the bedraggled army
Of bright-eyed, divine youths,
Who surged forward, who were driven back and
    fell,
Sick, broken, crying, shorn of faith,
Following the flag of the Kingdom of Heaven.
You and I, Harry Wilmans, have fallen
In our several ways, not knowing
Good from bad, defeat from victory,
Nor what face it is that smiles
Behind the demoniac mask.

LYMAN KING

You may think, passer-by, that Fate
Is a pit-fall outside of yourself,
Around which you may walk by the use of
     foresight
And wisdom.
Thus you believe, viewing the lives of other men,
As one who in God-like fashion bends over an
     anthill,
Seeing how their difficulties could be avoided.
But pass on into life:
In time you shall see Fate approach you
In the shape of your own image in the mirror;
Or you shall sit alone by your own hearth,
And suddenly the chair by you shall hold a guest,
And you shall know that guest,
And read the authentic message of his eyes.

CAROLINE BRANSON

With our hearts like drifting suns, had we but
    walked,
As often before, the April fields till star-light
Silkened over with viewless gauze the darkness
Under the cliff, our trysting place in the wood,
Where the brook turns! Had we but passed from
    wooing
Like notes of music that run together, into
    winning,
In the inspired improvisation of love!
But to put back of us as a canticle ended
The rapt enchantment of the flesh,
In which our souls swooned, down, down,
Where time was not, nor space, nor ourselves—
Annihilated in love!
To leave these behind for a room with lamps:
And to stand with our Secret mocking itself,
And hiding itself amid flowers and mandolins,
Stared at by all between salad and coffee.
And to see him tremble, and feel myself
Prescient, as one who signs a bond—
Not flaming with gifts and pledges heaped
With rosy hands over his brow.
And then, O night! deliberate! unlovely!
With all of our wooing blotted out by the winning,
In a chosen room in an hour that was known to
    all!
Next day he sat so listless, almost cold,
So strangely changed, wondering why I wept,
Till a kind of sick despair and voluptuous
    madness
Seized us to make the pact of death.

*   *   *

A stalk of the earth-sphere,
Frail as star-light;
Waiting to be drawn once again
Into creation's stream.
But next time to be given birth
Gazed at by Raphael and St. Francis
Sometimes as they pass.
For I am their little brother,
To be known clearly face to face
Through a cycle of birth hereafter run.
You may know the seed and the soil;
You may feel the cold rain fall,
But only the earth-sphere, only heaven
Knows the secret of the seed
In the nuptial chamber under the soil.
Throw me into the stream again,
Give me another trial—
Save me, Shelley!

ANNE RUTLEDGE*

Out of me unworthy and unknown
The vibrations of deathless music;
"With malice toward none, with charity for all."†
Out of me the forgiveness of millions toward
    millions,
And the beneficent face of a nation
Shining with justice and truth.
I am Anne Rutledge who sleep beneath these
    weeds,
Beloved in life of Abraham Lincoln,
Wedded to him, not through union,
But through separation.
Bloom forever, O Republic,
From the dust of my bosom!

---

*Anne Rutledge (1816–1835), popularly believed (perhaps because of Herndon's influence) to have been the great love of Lincoln's life who died of "brain fever"
†"With malice . . . all" the famous phrase from Lincoln's Second Inaugural Address, 1865

HAMLET MICURE

In a lingering fever many visions come to you:
I was in the little house again
With its great yard of clover
Running down to the board-fence,
Shadowed by the oak tree,
Where we children had our swing.
Yet the little house was a manor hall
Set in a lawn, and by the lawn was the sea.
I was in the room where little Paul
Strangled from diphtheria,
But yet it was not this room—
It was a sunny verandah enclosed
With mullioned windows,
And in a chair sat a man in a dark cloak,*
With a face like Euripides.
He had come to visit me, or I had gone to visit
    him—
I could not tell.
We could hear the beat of the sea, the clover
    nodded
Under a summer wind, and little Paul came
With clover blossoms to the window and smiled.
Then I said: "What is 'divine despair,' Alfred?"

*a man in a dark cloak** Alfred, Lord Tennyson; the poem alluded
to shortly after is the song, from *The Princess*, whose first stanza
Masters expected his readers to have in mind:

> Tears, idle tears, I know not what they mean,
> Tears from the depths of some divine despair
> Rise in the heart, and gather to the eyes
> In looking on the happy autumn fields
> And thinking of the days that are no more.

"Have you read 'Tears, Idle Tears'?" he asked.
"Yes, but you do not there express divine
    despair."
"My poor friend," he answered, "that was why
    the despair
Was divine."

MABEL OSBORNE

Your red blossoms amid green leaves
Are drooping, beautiful geranium!
But you do not ask for water.
You cannot speak! You do not need to speak—
Everyone knows that you are dying of thirst,
Yet they do not bring water!
They pass on, saying:
"The geranium wants water."
And I, who had happiness to share
And longed to share your happiness;
I who loved you, Spoon River,
And craved your love,
Withered before your eyes, Spoon River—
Thirsting, thirsting,
Voiceless from chasteness of soul to ask you for
     love,
You who knew and saw me perish before you,
Like this geranium which someone has planted
     over me,
And left to die.

WILLIAM H. HERNDON*

There by the window in the old house
Perched on the bluff, overlooking miles of valley,
My days of labor closed, sitting out life's decline,
Day by day did I look in my memory,
As one who gazes in an enchantress' crystal globe,
And I saw the figures of the past,
As if in a pageant glassed by a shining dream,
Move through the incredible sphere of time.
And I saw a man arise from the soil like a fa-
    bled giant
And throw himself over a deathless destiny,
Master of great armies, head of the republic,
Bringing together into a dithyramb of recreative
    song
The epic hopes of a people;
At the same time Vulcan of sovereign fires,
Where imperishable shields and swords were
    beaten out
From spirits tempered in heaven.
Look in the crystal! See how he hastens on
To the place where his path comes up to the path
Of a child of Plutarch and Shakespeare.
O Lincoln, actor indeed, playing well your part,
And Booth, who strode in a mimic play within
    the play,
Often and often I saw you,
As the cawing crows winged their way to the wood
Over my house-top at solemn sunsets,
There by my window,
Alone.

*William Henry Herndon (1818–1891) was Lincoln's law partner
and early biographer

REBECCA WASSON

Spring and Summer, Fall and Winter and Spring
After each other drifting, past my window
    drifting!
And I lay so many years watching them drift
    and counting
The years till a terror came in my heart at times,
With the feeling that I had become eternal; at last
My hundredth year was reached! And still I lay
Hearing the tick of the clock, and the low of cattle
And the scream of a jay flying through falling
    leaves!
Day after day alone in a room of the house
Of a daughter-in-law stricken with age and gray.
And by night, or looking out of the window by
    day
My thought ran back, it seemed, through infinite
    time
To North Carolina and all my girlhood days,
And John, my John, away to the war with the
    British,
And all the children, the deaths, and all the
    sorrows.
And that stretch of years like a prairie in Illinois
Through which great figures passed like hur-
    rying horsemen,
Washington, Jefferson, Jackson, Webster, Clay.
O beautiful young republic for whom my John
    and I
Gave all of our strength and love!
And O my John!
Why, when I lay so helpless in bed for years,

Praying for you to come, was your coming
    delayed?
Seeing that with a cry of rapture, like that I uttered
When you found me in old Virginia after the war,
I cried when I beheld you there by the bed,
As the sun stood low in the west growing smaller
    and fainter
In the light of your face!

RUTHERFORD McDOWELL

They brought me ambrotypes*
Of the old pioneers to enlarge.
And sometimes one sat for me—
Some one who was in being
When giant hands from the womb of the world
Tore the republic.
What was it in their eyes?—
For I could never fathom
That mystical pathos of drooped eyelids,
And the serene sorrow of their eyes.
It was like a pool of water,
Amid oak trees at the edge of a forest,
Where the leaves fall,
As you hear the crow of a cock
From a far-off farm house, seen near the hills
Where the third generation lives, and the strong
　　men
And the strong women are gone and forgotten.
And these grand-children and great grand-
　　children
Of the pioneers!
Truly did my camera record their faces, too,
With so much of the old strength gone,
And the old faith gone,
And the old mastery of life gone,
And the old courage gone,
Which labors and loves and suffers and sings
Under the sun!

*ambrotypes collodion print photographs

HANNAH ARMSTRONG*

I wrote him a letter asking him for old times' sake
To discharge my sick boy from the army;
But maybe he couldn't read it.
Then I went to town and had James Garber,
Who wrote beautifully, write him a letter;
But maybe that was lost in the mails.
So I traveled all the way to Washington.
I was more than an hour finding the White House.
And when I found it they turned me away,
Hiding their smiles. Then I thought:
"Oh, well, he ain't the same as when I boarded
      him
And he and my husband worked together
And all of us called him Abe, there in Menard."
As a last attempt I turned to a guard and said:
"Please say it's old Aunt Hannah Armstrong
From Illinois, come to see him about her sick boy
In the army."
Well, just in a moment they let me in!
And when he saw me he broke in a laugh,
And dropped his business as president,
And wrote in his own hand Doug's discharge,
Talking the while of the early days,
And telling stories.

*See Introduction, p. xx

LUCINDA MATLOCK*

I went to the dances at Chandlerville,
And played snap-out at Winchester.
One time we changed partners,
Driving home in the moonlight of middle June,
And then I found Davis.
We were married and lived together for seventy
     years,
Enjoying, working, raising the twelve children,
Eight of whom we lost
Ere I had reached the age of sixty.
I spun, I wove, I kept the house, I nursed the sick,
I made the garden, and for holiday
Rambled over the fields where sang the larks,
And by Spoon River gathering many a shell,
And many a flower and medicinal weed—
Shouting to the wooded hills, singing to the
     green valleys.
At ninety-six I had lived enough, that is all,
And passed to a sweet repose.
What is this I hear of sorrow and weariness,
Anger, discontent and drooping hopes?
Degenerate sons and daughters,
Life is too strong for you—
It takes life to love Life.

*See Introduction, p. xix

DAVIS MATLOCK*

Suppose it is nothing but the hive:
That there are drones and workers
And queens, and nothing but storing honey—
(Material things as well as culture and wisdom)—
For the next generation, this generation never
    living,
Except as it swarms in the sun-light of youth,
Strengthening its wings on what has been
    gathered,
And tasting, on the way to the hive
From the clover field, the delicate spoil.
Suppose all this, and suppose the truth:
That the nature of man is greater
Than nature's need in the hive;
And you must bear the burden of life,
As well as the urge from your spirit's excess—
Well, I say to live it out like a god
Sure of immortal life, though you are in doubt,
Is the way to live it.
If that doesn't make God proud of you
Then God is nothing but gravitation,
Or sleep is the golden goal.

*See Introduction, p. xix

HERMAN ALTMAN

Did I follow Truth wherever she led,
And stand against the whole world for a cause,
And uphold the weak against the strong?
If I did I would be remembered among men
As I was known in life among the people,
And as I was hated and loved on earth,
Therefore, build no monument to me,
And carve no bust for me,
Lest, though I become not a demi-god,
The reality of my soul be lost,
So that thieves and liars,
Who were my enemies and destroyed me,
And the children of thieves and liars,
May claim me and affirm before my bust
That they stood with me in the days of my defeat.
Build me no monument
Lest my memory be perverted to the uses
Of lying and oppression.
My lovers and their children must not be dispos-
    sessed of me;
I would be the untarnished possession forever
Of those for whom I lived.

JENNIE M'GREW

Not, where the stairway turns in the dark,
A hooded figure, shriveled under a flowing cloak!
Not yellow eyes in the room at night,
Staring out from a surface of cobweb gray!
And not the flap of a condor wing,
When the roar of life in your ears begins
As a sound heard never before!
But on a sunny afternoon,
By a country road,
Where purple rag-weeds bloom along a strag-
    gling fence,
And the field is gleaned, and the air is still,
To see against the sun-light something black,
Like a blot with an iris rim—
That is the sign to eyes of second sight. . . .
And that I saw!

COLUMBUS CHENEY

This weeping willow!
Why do you not plant a few
For the millions of children not yet born,
As well as for us?
Are they not non-existent, or cells asleep
Without mind?
Or do they come to earth, their birth
Rupturing the memory of previous being?
Answer! The field of unexplored intuition is yours,
But in any case why not plant willows for them,
As well as for us?

WALLACE FERGUSON

There at Geneva where Mt. Blanc floated above
The wine-hued lake like a cloud, when a breeze
    was blown
Out of an empty sky of blue, and the roaring
    Rhone
Hurried under the bridge through chasms of rock;
And the music along the cafés was part of the
    splendor
Of dancing water under a torrent of light;
And the purer part of the genius of Jean Rousseau
Was the silent music of all we saw or heard—
There at Geneva, I say, was the rapture less
Because I could not link myself with the I of yore,
When twenty years before I wandered about
    Spoon River?
Nor remember what I was nor what I felt?
We live in the hour all free of the hours gone by.
Therefore, O soul, if you lose yourself in death,
And wake in some Geneva by some Mt. Blanc,
What do you care if you know not yourself as
    the you
Who lived and loved in a little corner of earth
Known as Spoon River ages and ages vanished?

MARIE BATESON

You observe the carven hand
With the index finger pointing heavenward.
That is the direction, no doubt.
But how shall one follow it?
It is well to abstain from murder and lust,
To forgive, do good to others, worship God
Without graven images.
But these are external means after all
By which you chiefly do good to yourself.
The inner kernel is freedom.
It is light, purity—
I can no more,
Find the goal or lose it, according to your vision.

TENNESSEE CLAFLIN SHOPE

I was the laughing-stock of the village,
Chiefly of the people of good sense, as they call
    themselves—
Also of the learned, like Rev. Peet, who read Greek
The same as English.
For instead of talking free trade,
Or preaching some form of baptism;
Instead of believing in the efficacy
Of walking cracks, picking up pins the right way,
Seeing the new moon over the right shoulder,
Or curing rheumatism with blue glass,
I asserted the sovereignty of my own soul.
Before Mary Baker G. Eddy* even got started
With what she called science
I had mastered the "Bhagavad Gita,"†
And cured my soul, before Mary
Began to cure bodies with souls—
Peace to all worlds!

*__Mary Baker G. Eddy__ (1821–1910), better known as Mary Baker
Eddy, a Mr. Glover having been her husband for less than a year:
founder of the church of Christian Science
†__"Bhagavad Gita"__ "The Song of God," a widely known didactic
portion of the Indian epic the *Mahabharata*

PLYMOUTH ROCK JOE

Why are you running so fast hither and thither
Chasing midges or butterflies?
Some of you are standing solemnly scratching
     for grubs;
Some of you are waiting for corn to be scattered.
This is life, is it?
Cock-a-doodle-do! Very well, Thomas Rhodes,
You are cock of the walk no doubt.
But here comes Elliott Hawkins,
Gluck, Gluck, Gluck, attracting political followers.
Quah! quah! quah! why so poetical, Minerva,
This gray morning?
Kittie—quah—quah! for shame, Lucius Atherton,
The raucous squawk you evoked from the throat
Of Aner Clute will be taken up later
By Mrs. Benjamin Pantier as a cry
Of votes for women: Ka dook—dook!
What inspiration has come to you, Margaret Ful-
     ler Slack?
And why does your gooseberry eye
Flit so liquidly, Tennessee Claflin Shope?
Are you trying to fathom the esotericism of an egg?
Your voice is very metallic this morning, Hortense
     Robbins—
Almost like a guinea hen's!
Quah! That was a guttural sigh, Isaiah Beethoven;
Did you see the shadow of the hawk,
Or did you step upon the drumsticks
Which the cook threw out this morning?
Be chivalric, heroic, or aspiring,
Metaphysical, religious, or rebellious,
You shall never get out of the barnyard
Except by way of over the fence
Mixed with potato peelings and such into the trough!

IMANUEL EHRENHARDT

I began with Sir William Hamilton's* lectures.
Then studied Dugald Stewart;†
And then John Locke on the Understanding,
And then Descartes, Fichte and Schelling,
Kant and then Schopenhauer—
Books I borrowed from old Judge Somers.
All read with rapturous industry
Hoping it was reserved to me
To grasp the tail of the ultimate secret,
And drag it out of its hole.
My soul flew up ten thousand miles,
And only the moon looked a little bigger.
Then I fell back, how glad of the earth!
All through the soul of William Jones
Who showed me a letter of John Muir.‡

---

*William Hamilton** (1788–1856) and †**Dugald Stewart** (1753–1828),
Scottish philosophers
‡**John Muir** (1838–1914), American naturalist and writer

SAMUEL GARDNER

I who kept the greenhouse,
Lover of trees and flowers,
Oft in life saw this umbrageous elm,
Measuring its generous branches with my eye,
And listened to its rejoicing leaves
Lovingly patting each other
With sweet æolian whispers.
And well they might:
For the roots had grown so wide and deep
That the soil of the hill could not withhold
Aught of its virtue, enriched by rain,
And warmed by the sun;
But yielded it all to the thrifty roots,
Through which it was drawn and whirled to the
     trunk,
And thence to the branches, and into the leaves,
Wherefrom the breeze took life and sang.
Now I, an under-tenant of the earth, can see
That the branches of a tree
Spread no wider than its roots.
And how shall the soul of a man
Be larger than the life he has lived?

DOW KRITT

Samuel is forever talking of his elm—
But I did not need to die to learn about roots:
I, who dug all the ditches about Spoon River.
Look at my elm!
Sprung from as good a seed as his,
Sown at the same time,
It is dying at the top:
Not from lack of life, nor fungus,
Nor destroying insect, as the sexton thinks.
Look, Samuel, where the roots have struck rock
And can no further spread.
And all the while the top of the tree
Is tiring itself out, and dying,
Trying to grow.

WILLIAM JONES

Once in a while a curious weed unknown to me,
Needing a name from my books;
Once in a while a letter from Yeomans.*
Out of the mussel-shells gathered along the shore
Sometimes a pearl with a glint like meadow rue:
Then betimes a letter from Tyndall† in England,
Stamped with the stamp of Spoon River.
I, lover of Nature, beloved for my love of her,
Held such converse afar with the great
Who knew her better than I.
Oh, there is neither lesser nor greater,
Save as we make her greater and win from her
    keener delight.
With shells from the river cover me, cover me.
I lived in wonder, worshipping earth and heaven.
I have passed on the march eternal of endless life.

*Yeomans unidentified—but possibly a well-known nursery with
a widely distributed seed catalogue
†John Tyndall (1820–1893), Irish physicist

WILLIAM GOODE

To all in the village I seemed, no doubt,
To go this way and that way, aimlessly.
But here by the river you can see at twilight
The soft-winged bats fly zig-zag here and there—
They must fly so to catch their food.
And if you have ever lost your way at night,
In the deep wood near Miller's Ford,
And dodged this way and now that,
Wherever the light of the Milky Way shone
    through,
Trying to find the path,
You should understand I sought the way
With earnest zeal, and all my wanderings
Were wanderings in the quest.

J. MILTON MILES

Whenever the Presbyterian bell
Was rung by itself, I knew it as the Presbyterian
    bell.
But when its sound was mingled
With the sound of the Methodist, the Christian,
The Baptist and the Congregational,
I could no longer distinguish it,
Nor any one from the others, or either of them.
And as many voices called to me in life
Marvel not that I could not tell
The true from the false,
Nor even, at last, the voice that I should have
    known.

FAITH MATHENY

At first you will know not what they mean,
And you may never know,
And we may never tell you:—
These sudden flashes in your soul,
Like lambent lightning on snowy clouds
At midnight when the moon is full.
They come in solitude, or perhaps
You sit with your friend, and all at once
A silence falls on speech, and his eyes
Without a flicker glow at you:—
You two have seen the secret together,
He sees it in you, and you in him.
And there you sit thrilling lest the Mystery
Stand before you and strike you dead
With a splendor like the sun's.
Be brave, all souls who have such visions!
As your body's alive as mine is dead,
You're catching a little whiff of the ether
Reserved for God Himself.

SCHOLFIELD HUXLEY

God! ask me not to record your wonders,
I admit the stars and the suns
And the countless worlds.
But I have measured their distances
And weighed them and discovered their
    substances.
I have devised wings for the air,
And keels for water,
And horses of iron for the earth.
I have lengthened the vision you gave me a mil-
    lion times,
And the hearing you gave me a million times,
I have leaped over space with speech,
And taken fire for light out of the air.
I have built great cities and bored through the
    hills,
And bridged majestic waters.
I have written the Iliad and Hamlet;
And I have explored your mysteries,
And searched for you without ceasing,
And found you again after losing you
In hours of weariness—
And I ask you:
How would you like to create a sun
And the next day have the worms
Slipping in and out between your fingers?

WILLIE METCALF

I was Willie Metcalf.
They used to call me "Doctor Meyers"
Because, they said, I looked like him.
And he was my father, according to Jack McGuire.
I lived in the livery stable,
Sleeping on the floor
Side by side with Roger Baughman's bulldog,
Or sometimes in a stall.
I could crawl between the legs of the wildest
     horses
Without getting kicked—we knew each other.
On spring days I tramped through the country
To get the feeling, which I sometimes lost,
That I was not a separate thing from the earth.
I used to lose myself, as if in sleep,
By lying with eyes half-open in the woods.
Sometimes I talked with animals—even toads and
     snakes—
Anything that had an eye to look into.
Once I saw a stone in the sunshine
Trying to turn into jelly.
In April days in this cemetery
The dead people gathered all about me,
And grew still, like a congregation in silent prayer.
I never knew whether I was a part of the earth
With flowers growing in me or whether I
     walked—
Now I know.

WILLIE PENNINGTON

They called me the weakling, the simpleton,
For my brothers were strong and beautiful,
While I, the last child of parents who had aged,
Inherited only their residue of power.
But they, my brothers, were eaten up
In the fury of the flesh, which I had not,
Made pulp in the activity of the senses, which I
    had not,
Hardened by the growth of the lusts, which I
    had not,
Though making names and riches for themselves.
Then I, the weak one, the simpleton,
Resting in a little corner of life,
Saw a vision, and through me many saw the
    vision,
Not knowing it was through me.
Thus a tree sprang
From me, a mustard seed.

THE VILLAGE ATHEIST

Ye young debaters over the doctrine
Of the soul's immortality,
I who lie here was the village atheist,
Talkative, contentious, versed in the arguments
Of the infidels.
But through a long sickness
Coughing myself to death
I read the *Upanishads** and the poetry of Jesus.
And they lighted a torch of hope and intuition
And desire which the Shadow,
Leading me swiftly through the caverns of
    darkness,
Could not extinguish.
Listen to me, ye who live in the senses
And think through the senses only:
Immortality is not a gift,
Immortality is an achievement;
And only those who strive mightily
Shall possess it.

---

*Upanishads ancient Sanskrit philosophical treatises central to
Hindu religion and thought

JOHN BALLARD

In the lust of my strength
I cursed God, but he paid no attention to me:
I might as well have cursed the stars.
In my last sickness I was in agony, but I was
     resolute
And I cursed God for my suffering;
Still He paid no attention to me;
He left me alone, as He had always done.
I might as well have cursed the Presbyterian
     steeple.
Then, as I grew weaker, a terror came over me:
Perhaps I had alienated God by cursing him.
One day Lydia Humphrey brought me a bouquet
And it occurred to me to try to make friends
     with God,
So I tried to make friends with Him;
But I might as well have tried to make friends
     with the bouquet.
Now I was very close to the secret,
For I really could make friends with the bouquet
By holding close to me the love in me for the
     bouquet
And so I was creeping upon the secret, but—

JULIAN SCOTT

Toward the last
The truth of others was untruth to me;
The justice of others injustice to me;
Their reasons for death, reasons with me for life;
Their reasons for life, reasons with me for death;
I would have killed those they saved,
And saved those they killed.
And I saw how a god, if brought to earth,
Must act out what he saw and thought,
And could not live in this world of men
And act among them side by side
Without continual clashes.
The dust's for crawling, heaven's for flying—
Wherefore, O soul, whose wings are grown,
Soar upward to the sun!

ALFONSO CHURCHILL

They laughed at me as "Prof. Moon,"
As a boy in Spoon River, born with the thirst
Of knowing about the stars.
They jeered when I spoke of the lunar mountains,
And the thrilling heat and cold,
And the ebon valleys by silver peaks,
And Spica quadrillions of miles away,
And the littleness of man.
But now that my grave is honored, friends,
Let it not be because I taught
The lore of the stars in Knox College,
But rather for this: that through the stars
I preached the greatness of man,
Who is none the less a part of the scheme of things
For the distance of Spica or the Spiral Nebulæ;
Nor any the less a part of the question
Of what the drama means.

ZILPHA MARSH

At four o'clock in late October
I sat alone in the country school-house
Back from the road 'mid stricken fields,
And an eddy of wind blew leaves on the pane,
And crooned in the flue of the cannon-stove,
With its open door blurring the shadows
With the spectral glow of a dying fire.
In an idle mood I was running the planchette*—
All at once my wrist grew limp,
And my hand moved rapidly over the board,
Till the name of "Charles Guiteau"† was spelled,
Who threatened to materialize before me.
I rose and fled from the room bare-headed
Into the dusk, afraid of my gift.
And after that the spirits swarmed—
Chaucer, Cæsar, Poe and Marlowe,
Cleopatra and Mrs. Surrat‡—
Wherever I went, with messages,—
Mere trifling twaddle, Spoon River agreed.
You talk nonsense to children, don't you?
And suppose I see what you never saw
And never heard of and have no word for,
I must talk nonsense when you ask me
What it is I see!

---

*planchette small triangular board on casters with a pencil affixed
to it, supposedly to spell out messages from the spirit-world;
today, this would be used on a so-called "ouija board"
†Charles Guiteau (1840–1882), hanged for assassinating President
James A. Garfield
‡Mrs. Surrat Mary E. Surrat (1820–1865), likewise hanged for con-
spiracy in the plot to execute Lincoln

JAMES GARBER

Do you remember, passer-by, the path
I wore across the lot where now stands the
    opera house,
Hasting with swift feet to work through many
    years?
Take its meaning to heart:
You too may walk, after the hills at Miller's Ford
Seem no longer far away;
Long after you see them near at hand,
Beyond four miles of meadow;
And after woman's love is silent,
Saying no more: "I will save you."
And after the faces of friends and kindred
Become as faded photographs, pitifully silent,
Sad for the look which means: "We cannot help
    you."
And after you no longer reproach mankind
With being in league against your soul's uplifted
    hands—
Themselves compelled at midnight and at noon
To watch with steadfast eye their destinies;
After you have these understandings, think of me
And of my path, who walked therein and knew
That neither man nor woman, neither toil,
Nor duty, gold nor power
Can ease the longing of the soul,
The loneliness of the soul!

LYDIA HUMPHREY

Back and forth, back and forth to and from the
    church,
With my Bible under my arm
Till I was gray and old;
Unwedded, alone in the world,
Finding brothers and sisters in the congregation,
And children in the church.
I know they laughed and thought me queer.
I knew of the eagle souls that flew high in the
    sunlight,
Above the spire of the church, and laughed at
    the church,
Disdaining me, not seeing me.
But if the high air was sweet to them, sweet was
    the church to me.
It was the vision, vision, vision of the poets
Democratized!

LE ROY GOLDMAN

"What will you do when you come to die,
If all your life long you have rejected Jesus,
And know as you lie there, He is not your friend?"
Over and over I said, I, the revivalist.
Ah, yes! but there are friends and friends.
And blessed are you, say I, who know all now,
You who have lost, ere you pass,
A father or mother, or old grandfather or mother,
Some beautiful soul that lived life strongly,
And knew you all through, and loved you ever,
Who would not fail to speak for you,
And give God an intimate view of your soul,
As only one of your flesh could do it.
That is the hand your hand will reach for,
To lead you along the corridor
To the court where you are a stranger!

GUSTAV RICHTER

After a long day of work in my hot-houses
Sleep was sweet, but if you sleep on your left side
Your dreams may be abruptly ended.
I was among my flowers where some one
Seemed to be raising them on trial,
As if after-while to be transplanted
To a larger garden of freer air.
And I was disembodied vision
Amid a light, as it were the sun
Had floated in and touched the roof of glass
Like a toy balloon and softly bursted,
And etherealized in golden air.
And all was silence, except the splendor
Was immanent with thought as clear
As a speaking voice, and I, as thought,
Could hear a Presence think as he walked
Between the boxes pinching off leaves,
Looking for bugs and noting values,
With an eye that saw it all:—
"Homer, oh yes! Pericles, good.
Cæsar Borgia, what shall be done with it?
Dante, too much manure, perhaps.
Napoleon, leave him awhile as yet.
Shelley, more soil. Shakespeare, needs spraying—"
Clouds, eh!—

ARLO WILL

Did you ever see an alligator
Come up to the air from the mud,
Staring blindly under the full glare of noon?
Have you seen the stabled horses at night
Tremble and start back at the sight of a lantern?
Have you ever walked in darkness
When an unknown door was open before you
And you stood, it seemed, in the light of a thou-
      sand candles
Of delicate wax?
Have you walked with the wind in your ears
And the sunlight about you
And found it suddenly shine with an inner
      splendor?
Out of the mud many times,
Before many doors of light,
Through many fields of splendor,
Where around your steps a soundless glory
      scatters
Like new-fallen snow,
Will you go through earth, O strong of soul,
And through unnumbered heavens
To the final flame!

CAPTAIN ORLANDO KILLION

Oh, you young radicals and dreamers,
You dauntless fledglings
Who pass by my headstone,
Mock not its record of my captaincy in the army
And my faith in God!
They are not denials of each other.
Go by reverently, and read with sober care
How a great people, riding with defiant shouts
The centaur of Revolution,
Spurred and whipped to frenzy,
Shook with terror, seeing the mist of the sea
Over the precipice they were nearing,
And fell from his back in precipitate awe
To celebrate the Feast of the Supreme Being.*
Moved by the same sense of vast reality
Of life and death, and burdened as they were
With the fate of a race,
How was I, a little blasphemer,
Caught in the drift of a nation's unloosened flood,
To remain a blasphemer,
And a captain in the army?

---

*Feast of the Supreme Being** in the French Revolutionary Calendar, a secular replacement for Christian festivals

JEREMY CARLISLE

Passer-by, sin beyond any sin
Is the sin of blindness of souls to other souls.
And joy beyond any joy is the joy
Of having the good in you seen, and seeing the
        good
At the miraculous moment!
Here I confess to a lofty scorn,
And an acrid skepticism.
But do you remember the liquid that Penniwit
Poured on tintypes, making them blue
With a mist like hickory smoke?
Then how the picture began to clear
Till the face came forth like life?
So you appeared to me, neglected ones,
And enemies too, as I went along
With my face growing clearer to you as yours
Grew clearer to me.
We were ready then to walk together
And sing in chorus and chant the dawn
Of life that is wholly life.

JOSEPH DIXON

Who carved this shattered harp on my stone?
I died to you, no doubt. But how many harps
    and pianos
Wired I and tightened and disentangled for you,
Making them sweet again—with tuning fork or
    without?
Oh well! A harp leaps out of the ear of a man,
    you say,
But whence the ear that orders the length of the
    strings
To a magic of numbers flying before your thought
Through a door that closes against your breath-
    less wonder?
Is there no Ear round the ear of a man, that it
    senses
Through strings and columns of air the soul of
    sound?
I thrill as I call it a tuning fork that catches
The waves of mingled music and light from afar,
The antennæ of Thought that listens through ut-
    most space.
Surely the concord that ruled my spirit is proof
Of an Ear that tuned me, able to tune me over
And use me again if I am worthy to use.

JUDSON STODDARD

On a mountain top above the clouds
That streamed like a sea below me
I said that peak is the thought of Buddha,
And that one is the prayer of Jesus,
And this one is the dream of Plato,
And that one there the song of Dante,
And this is Kant and this is Newton,
And this is Milton and this is Shakespeare,
And this the hope of the Mother Church,
And this—why all these peaks are poems,
Poems and prayers that pierce the clouds.
And I said "What does God do with mountains
That rise almost to heaven?"

RUSSELL KINCAID

In the last spring I ever knew,
In those last days,
I sat in the forsaken orchard
Where beyond fields of greenery shimmered
The hills at Miller's Ford;
Just to muse on the apple tree
With its ruined trunk and blasted branches,
And shoots of green whose delicate blossoms
Were sprinkled over the skeleton tangle,
Never to grow in fruit.
And there was I with my spirit girded
By the flesh half dead, the senses numb,
Yet thinking of youth and the earth in youth,—
Such phantom blossoms palely shining
Over the lifeless boughs of Time.
O earth that leaves us ere heaven takes us!
Had I been only a tree to shiver
With dreams of spring and a leafy youth,
Then I had fallen in the cyclone
Which swept me out of the soul's suspense
Where it's neither earth nor heaven.

AARON HATFIELD

Better than granite, Spoon River,
Is the memory-picture you keep of me
Standing before the pioneer men and women
There at Concord Church on Communion day.
Speaking in broken voice of the peasant youth
Of Galilee who went to the city
And was killed by bankers and lawyers;
My voice mingling with the June wind
That blew over wheat fields from Atterbury;
While the white stones in the burying ground
Around the Church shimmered in the summer
    sun.
And there, though my own memories
Were too great to bear, were you, O pioneers,*
With bowed heads breathing forth your sorrow
For the sons killed in battle and the daughters
And little children who vanished in life's morning,
Or at the intolerable hour of noon.
But in those moments of tragic silence,
When the wine and bread were passed,
Came the reconciliation for us—
Us the ploughmen and the hewers of wood,
Us the peasants, brothers of the peasant of
    Galilee—
To us came the Comforter
And the consolation of tongues of flame!†

---

*O pioneers the phrase is Whitman's
†tongues of flame see Acts, 2:1–4

ISAIAH BEETHOVEN

They told me I had three months to live,
So I crept to Bernadotte,
And sat by the mill for hours and hours
Where the gathered waters deeply moving
Seemed not to move:
O world, that's you!
You are but a widened place in the river
Where Life looks down and we rejoice for her
Mirrored in us, and so we dream
And turn away, but when again
We look for the face, behold the low-lands
And blasted cotton-wood trees where we empty
Into the larger stream!
But here by the mill the castled clouds
Mocked themselves in the dizzy water;
And over its agate floor at night
The flame of the moon ran under my eyes
Amid a forest stillness broken
By a flute in a hut on the hill.
At last when I came to lie in bed
Weak and in pain, with the dreams about me,
The soul of the river had entered my soul,
And the gathered power of my soul was moving
So swiftly it seemed to be at rest
Under cities of cloud and under
Spheres of silver and changing worlds—
Until I saw a flash of trumpets
Above the battlements over Time!

ELIJAH BROWNING

I was among multitudes of children
Dancing at the foot of a mountain.
A breeze blew out of the east and swept them
    as leaves,
Driving some up the slopes. . . . All was changed.
Here were flying lights, and mystic moons, and
    dream-music.
A cloud fell upon us. When it lifted all was
    changed.
I was now amid multitudes who were wrangling.
Then a figure in shimmering gold, and one with
    a trumpet,
And one with a sceptre stood before me.
They mocked me and danced a rigadoon and
    vanished. . . .
All was changed again. Out of a bower of poppies
A woman bared her breasts and lifted her open
    mouth to mine.
I kissed her. The taste of her lips was like salt.
She left blood on my lips. I fell exhausted.
I arose and ascended higher, but a mist as from
    an iceberg
Clouded my steps. I was cold and in pain.
Then the sun streamed on me again,
And I saw the mists below me hiding all below
    them.
And I, bent over my staff, knew myself
Silhouetted against the snow. And above me
Was the soundless air, pierced by a cone of ice,
Over which hung a solitary star!
A shudder of ecstasy, a shudder of fear

Ran through me. But I could not return to the
    slopes—
Nay, I wished not to return.
For the spent waves of the symphony of freedom
Lapped the ethereal cliffs about me.
Therefore I climbed to the pinnacle.
I flung away my staff.
I touched that star
With my outstretched hand.
I vanished utterly.
For the mountain delivers to Infinite Truth
Whosoever touches the star!

WEBSTER FORD*

Do you remember, O Delphic Apollo,
The sunset hour by the river, when Mickey
    M'Grew
Cried, "There's a ghost," and I, "It's Delphic
    Apollo";
And the son of the banker derided us, saying,
    "It's light
By the flags at the water's edge, you half-witted
    fools."
And from thence, as the wearisome years rolled
    on, long after
Poor Mickey fell down in the water tower to his
    death,
Down, down, through bellowing darkness, I
    carried
The vision which perished with him like a rocket
    which falls
And quenches its light in earth, and hid it for fear
Of the son of the banker, calling on Plutus to
    save me?
Avenged were you for the shame of a fearful
    heart,
Who left me alone till I saw you again in an hour
When I seemed to be turned to a tree with trunk
    and branches
Growing indurate, turning to stone, yet
    burgeoning
In laurel leaves, in hosts of lambent laurel,

*Masters himself; the Ovidian myth of Daphne and Apollo is a
fable of the origins of poetry in defeated erotic desire

Quivering, fluttering, shrinking, fighting the
    numbness
Creeping into their veins from the dying trunk
    and branches!
'Tis vain, O youth, to fly the call of Apollo.
Fling yourselves in the fire, die with a song of
    spring,
If die you must in the spring. For none shall look
On the face of Apollo and live, and choose you
    must
'Twixt death in the flame and death after years
    of sorrow,
Rooted fast in the earth, feeling the grisly hand,
Not so much in the trunk as in the terrible
    numbness
Creeping up to the laurel leaves that never cease
To flourish until you fall. O leaves of me
Too sere for coronal wreaths, and fit alone
For urns of memory, treasured, perhaps, as themes
For hearts heroic, fearless singers and livers—
Delphic Apollo!

THE SPOONIAD

[*The late Mr. Jonathan Swift Somers, laureate of Spoon River (see page 134), planned* The Spooniad *as an epic in twenty-four books, but unfortunately did not live to complete even the first book. The fragment was found among his papers by William Marion Reedy and was for the first time published in Reedy's* Mirror *of December 18th, 1914.*]

THE SPOONIAD

Of John Cabanis' wrath and of the strife
Of hostile parties, and his dire defeat
Who led the common people in the cause
Of freedom for Spoon River, and the fall
Of Rhodes' bank that brought unnumbered woes
And loss to many, with engendered hate
That flamed into the torch in Anarch hands
To burn the court-house, on whose blackened wreck
A fairer temple rose and Progress stood—
Sing, muse, that lit the Chian's face with smiles
Who saw the ant-like Greeks and Trojans crawl
About Scamander, over walls, pursued
Or else pursuing, and the funeral pyres
And sacred hecatombs, and first because
Of Helen who with Paris fled to Troy
As soul-mate; and the wrath of Peleus' son,
Decreed, to lose Chryseis, lovely spoil
Of war, and dearest concubine.
                                Say first,
Thou son of night, called Momus, from whose eyes
No secret hides, and Thalia, smiling one,
What bred 'twixt Thomas Rhodes and John
    Cabanis
The deadly strife? His daughter Flossie, she,
Returning from her wandering with a troop
Of strolling players, walked the village streets,
Her bracelets tinkling and with sparkling rings
And words of serpent wisdom and a smile
Of cunning in her eyes. Then Thomas Rhodes,
Who ruled the church and ruled the bank as well,
Made known his disapproval of the maid;
And all Spoon River whispered and the eyes
Of all the church frowned on her, till she knew
They feared her and condemned.

267

                                   But them to flout
She gave a dance to viols and to flutes,
Brought from Peoria, and many youths,
But lately made regenerate through the prayers
Of zealous preachers and of earnest souls,
Danced merrily, and sought her in the dance,
Who wore a dress so low of neck that eyes
Down straying might survey the snowy swale
Till it was lost in whiteness.
                                   With the dance
The village changed to merriment from gloom.
The milliner, Mrs. Williams, could not fill
Her orders for new hats, and every seamstress
Plied busy needles making gowns; old trunks
And chests were opened for their store of laces
And rings and trinkets were brought out of hiding
And all the youths fastidious grew of dress;
Notes passed, and many a fair one's door at eve
Knew a bouquet, and strolling lovers thronged
About the hills that overlooked the river.
Then, since the mercy seats more empty showed,
One of God's chosen lifted up his voice:
"The woman of Babylon is among us; rise
Ye sons of light and drive the wanton forth!"
So John Cabanis left the church and left
The hosts of law and order with his eyes
By anger cleared, and him the liberal cause
Acclaimed as nominee to the mayoralty
To vanquish A. D. Blood.
                                   But as the war
Waged bitterly for votes and rumors flew
About the bank, and of the heavy loans
Which Rhodes' son had made to prop his loss
In wheat, and many drew their coin and left
The bank of Rhodes more hollow, with the talk
Among the liberals of another bank
Soon to be chartered, lo, the bubble burst
'Mid cries and curses; but the liberals laughed
And in the hall of Nicholas Bindle held

Wise converse and inspiriting debate.
High on a stage that overlooked the chairs
Where dozens sat, and where a pop-eyed daub
Of Shakespeare, very like the hired man
Of Christian Dallman, brow and pointed beard,
Upon a drab proscenium outward stared,
Sat Harmon Whitney, to that eminence,
By merit raised in ribaldry and guile,
And to the assembled rebels thus he spake:
"Whether to lie supine and let a clique
Cold-blooded, scheming, hungry, singing psalms,
Devour our substance, wreck our banks and drain
Our little hoards for hazards on the price
Of wheat or pork, or yet to cower beneath
The shadow of a spire upreared to curb
A breed of lackeys and to serve the bank
Coadjutor in greed, that is the question.
Shall we have music and the jocund dance,
Or tolling bells? Or shall young romance roam
These hills about the river, flowering now
To April's tears, or shall they sit at home,
Or play croquet where Thomas Rhodes may see,
I ask you? If the blood of youth runs o'er
And riots 'gainst this regimen of gloom,
Shall we submit to have these youths and maids
Branded as libertines and wantons?"

                                        Ere
His words were done a woman's voice called
    "No!"
Then rose a sound of moving chairs, as when
The numerous swine o'er-run the replenished
    troughs;
And every head was turned, as when a flock
Of geese back-turning to the hunter's tread
Rise up with flapping wings; then rang the hall
With riotous laughter, for with battered hat
Tilted upon her saucy head, and fist
Raised in defiance, Daisy Fraser stood.
Headlong she had been hurled from out the hall

Save Wendell Bloyd, who spoke for woman's
　　　rights,
Prevented, and the bellowing voice of Burchard.
Then 'mid applause she hastened toward the stage
And flung both gold and silver to the cause
And swiftly left the hall.
　　　　　　　　　　　　Meantime upstood
A giant figure, bearded like the son
Of Alcmene, deep-chested, round of paunch,
And spoke in thunder: "Over there behold
A man who for the truth withstood his wife—
Such is our spirit—when that A. D. Blood
Compelled me to remove Dom Pedro—"
　　　　　　　　　　　　　　　　Quick
Before Jim Brown could finish Jefferson Howard
Obtained the floor and spake: "Ill suits the time
For clownish words, and trivial is our cause
If naught's at stake but John Cabanis' wrath,
He who was erstwhile of the other side
And came to us for vengeance. More's at stake
Than triumph for New England or Virginia.
And whether rum be sold, or for two years
As in the past two years, this town be dry
Matters but little—Oh yes, revenue
For sidewalks, sewers; that is well enough!
I wish to God this fight were now inspired
By other passion than to salve the pride
Of John Cabanis or his daughter. Why
Can never contests of great moment spring
From worthy things, not little? Still, if men
Must always act so, and if rum must be
The symbol and the medium to release
From life's denial and from slavery,
Then give me rum!"
　　　　　　　　　　　Exultant cries arose.
Then, as George Trimble had o'ercome his fear
And vacillation and begun to speak,
The door creaked and the idiot, Willie Metcalf,
Breathless and hatless, whiter than a sheet,

Entered and cried: "The marshal's on his way
To arrest you all. And if you only knew
Who's coming here to-morrow; I was listening
Beneath the window where the other side
Are making plans."
               So to a smaller room
To hear the idiot's secret some withdrew
Selected by the Chair; the Chair himself
And Jefferson Howard, Benjamin Pantier,
And Wendell Bloyd, George Trimble, Adam
    Weirauch,
Imanuel Ehrenhardt, Seth Compton, Godwin
    James
And Enoch Dunlap, Hiram Scates, Roy Butler,
Carl Hamblin, Roger Heston, Ernest Hyde
And Penniwit, the artist, Kinsey Keene,
And E. C. Culbertson and Franklin Jones,
Benjamin Fraser, son of Benjamin Pantier
By Daisy Fraser, some of lesser note,
And secretly conferred.
              But in the hall
Disorder reigned and when the marshal came
And found it so, he marched the hoodlums out
And locked them up.

              Meanwhile within a room
Back in the basement of the church, with Blood
Counseled the wisest heads. Judge Somers first,
Deep learned in life, and next him, Elliott Hawkins
And Lambert Hutchins; next him Thomas Rhodes
And Editor Whedon; next him Garrison Standard,
A traitor to the liberals, who with lip
Upcurled in scorn and with a bitter sneer:
"Such strife about an insult to a woman—
A girl of eighteen"—Christian Dallman too,
And others unrecorded. Some there were
Who frowned not on the cup but loathed the rule
Democracy achieved thereby, the freedom
And lust of life it symbolized.

*   *   *

Now morn with snowy fingers up the sky
Flung like an orange at a festival
The ruddy sun, when from their hasty beds
Poured forth the hostile forces, and the streets
Resounded to the rattle of the wheels,
That drove this way and that to gather in
The tardy voters, and the cries of chieftains
Who manned the battle. But at ten o'clock
The liberals bellowed fraud, and at the polls
The rival candidates growled and came to blows.
Then proved the idiot's tale of yester-eve
A word of warning. Suddenly on the streets
Walked hog-eyed Allen, terror of the hills
That looked on Bernadotte ten miles removed.
No man of this degenerate day could lift
The boulders which he threw, and when he spoke
The windows rattled, and beneath his brows,
Thatched like a shed with bristling hair of black,
His small eyes glistened like a maddened boar.
And as he walked the boards creaked, as he
     walked
A song of menace rumbled. Thus he came,
The champion of A. D. Blood, commissioned
To terrify the liberals. Many fled
As when a hawk soars o'er the chicken yard.
He passed the polls and with a playful hand
Touched Brown, the giant, and he fell against,
As though he were a child, the wall; so strong
Was hog-eyed Allen. But the liberals smiled.
For soon as hog-eyed Allen reached the walk,
Close on his steps paced Bengal Mike, brought in
By Kinsey Keene, the subtle-witted one,
To match the hog-eyed Allen. He was scarce
Three-fourths the other's bulk, but steel his arms,
And with a tiger's heart. Two men he killed
And many wounded in the days before,
And no one feared.

                    But when the hog-eyed one
Saw Bengal Mike his countenance grew dark,

The bristles o'er his red eyes twitched with rage,
The song he rumbled lowered. Round and round
The court-house paced he, followed stealthily
By Bengal Mike, who jeered him every step:
"Come, elephant, and fight! Come, hog-eyed
    coward!
Come, face about and fight me, lumbering sneak!
Come, beefy bully, hit me, if you can!
Take out your gun, you duffer, give me reason
To draw and kill you. Take your billy out;
I'll crack your boar's head with a piece of brick!"
But never a word the hog-eyed one returned,
But trod about the court-house, followed both
By troops of boys and watched by all the men.
All day, they walked the square. But when Apollo
Stood with reluctant look above the hills
As fain to see the end, and all the votes
Were cast, and closed the polls, before the door
Of Trainor's drug store Bengal Mike, in tones
That echoed through the village, bawled the taunt:
"Who was your mother, hog-eyed?" In a trice,
As when a wild boar turns upon the hound
That through the brakes upon an August day
Has gashed him with its teeth, the hog-eyed one
Rushed with his giant arms on Bengal Mike
And grabbed him by the throat. Then rose to
    heaven
The frightened cries of boys, and yells of men
Forth rushing to the street. And Bengal Mike
Moved this way and now that, drew in his head
As if his neck to shorten, and bent down
To break the death grip of the hog-eyed one;
'Twixt guttural wrath and fast-expiring strength
Striking his fists against the invulnerable chest
Of hog-eyed Allen. Then, when some came in
To part them, others stayed them, and the fight
Spread among dozens; many valiant souls
Went down from clubs and bricks.

                              But tell me, Muse,
What god or goddess rescued Bengal Mike?
With one last, mighty struggle did he grasp
The murderous hands and turning kick his foe.
Then, as if struck by lightning, vanished all
The strength from hog-eyed Allen, at his side
Sank limp those giant arms and o'er his face
Dread pallor and the sweat of anguish spread.
And those great knees, invincible but late,
Shook to his weight. And quickly as the lion
Leaps on its wounded prey, did Bengal Mike
Smite with a rock the temple of his foe,
And down he sank and darkness o'er his eyes
Passed like a cloud.

                              As when the woodman fells
Some giant oak upon a summer's day
And all the songsters of the forest shrill,
And one great hawk that has his nestling young
Amid the topmost branches croaks, as crash
The leafy branches through the tangled boughs
Of brother oaks, so fell the hog-eyed one
Amid the lamentations of the friends
Of A. D. Blood.

                              Just then, four lusty men
Bore the town marshal, on whose iron face
The purple pall of death already lay,
To Trainor's drug store, shot by Jack McGuire.
And cries went up of "Lynch him!" and the sound
Of running feet from every side was heard
Bent on the

EPILOGUE

(THE GRAVEYARD OF SPOON RIVER. TWO VOICES ARE HEARD
    BEHIND A SCREEN DECORATED WITH DIABOLICAL AND
    ANGELIC FIGURES IN VARIOUS ALLEGORICAL RELATIONS.
    A FAINT LIGHT SHOWS DIMLY THROUGH THE SCREEN AS IF
    IT WERE WOVEN OF LEAVES, BRANCHES AND SHADOWS.)

FIRST VOICE

A game of checkers?

SECOND VOICE

Well, I don't mind.

FIRST VOICE

I move the Will.

SECOND VOICE

You're playing it
blind.

FIRST VOICE

Then here's the Soul.

SECOND VOICE

Checked by the Will.

FIRST VOICE

Eternal Good!

SECOND VOICE

And Eternal ill.

FIRST VOICE

I haste for the King row.

SECOND VOICE

Save your breath.

FIRST VOICE

I was moving Life.

SECOND VOICE

You're checked by Death.

FIRST VOICE

Very good, here's Moses.

SECOND VOICE

And here's the Jew.

FIRST VOICE

My next move is Jesus.

SECOND VOICE

St. Paul for you!

FIRST VOICE

Yes, but St. Peter—

SECOND VOICE

You might have foreseen—

FIRST VOICE

You're in the King row—

SECOND VOICE

With Constantine!

FIRST VOICE

I'll go back to Athens.

SECOND VOICE
Well, here's the Persian.

FIRST VOICE
All right, the Bible.

SECOND VOICE
Pray now, what version?

FIRST VOICE
I take up Buddha.

SECOND VOICE
It never will work.

FIRST VOICE
From the corner Mahomet.

SECOND VOICE
I move the Turk.

FIRST VOICE
The game is tangled; where are we now?

SECOND VOICE
You're dreaming worlds. I'm in the King row.
Move as you will, if I can't wreck you
I'll thwart you, harry you, rout you, check you.

FIRST VOICE
I'm tired. I'll send for my Son to play.
I think he can beat you finally—

SECOND VOICE
Eh?

FIRST VOICE
I must preside at the stars' convention.

SECOND VOICE

Very well, my lord, but I beg to mention
I'll give this game my direct attention.

FIRST VOICE

A game indeed! But Truth is my quest.

SECOND VOICE

Beaten, you walk away with a jest.
I strike the table, I scatter the checkers.

(*A rattle of a falling table and checkers flying over a floor.*)

Aha! You armies and iron deckers,
Races and states in a cataclysm—
Now for a day of atheism!

(*The screen vanishes and* BEELZEBUB *steps forward carrying a trumpet, which he blows faintly. Immediately* LOKI *and* YOGARINDRA *start up from the shadows of night.*)

BEELZEBUB

Good evening, Loki!

LOKI

         The same to you!

BEELZEBUB

And Yogarindra!

YOGARINDRA

         My greetings, too.

LOKI

Whence came you, comrade?

BEELZEBUB

         From yonder screen.

YOGARINDRA

And what were you doing?

BEELZEBUB
                    Stirring His spleen.

LOKI

How did you do it?

BEELZEBUB
                    I made it rough
In a game of checkers.

LOKI
                    Good enough!

YOGARINDRA

I thought I heard the sounds of a battle.

BEELZEBUB

No doubt! I made the checkers rattle,
Turning the table over and strewing
The bits of wood like an army pursuing.

YOGARINDRA

I have a game! Let us make a man.

LOKI

My net is waiting him, if you can.

YOGARINDRA

And here's my mirror to fool him with—

BEELZEBUB

Mystery, falsehood, creed and myth.

LOKI

But no one can mold him, friend, but you.

BEELZEBUB

Then to the sport without more ado.

YOGARINDRA

Hurry the work ere it grow to day.

BEELZEBUB

I set me to it. Where is the clay?

(*He scrapes the earth with his hands and begins to model.*)

BEELZEBUB

Out of the dust,
Out of the slime,
A little rust,
And a little lime.
Muscle and gristle,
Mucin, stone
Brayed with a pestle,
Fat and bone.
Out of the marshes,
Out of the vaults,
Matter crushes
Gas and salts.
What is this you call a mind,
Flitting, drifting, pale and blind,
Soul of the swamp that rides the wind?
Jack-o'-lantern, here you are!
Dream of heaven, pine for a star,
Chase your brothers to and fro,
Back to the swamp at last you'll go.
Hilloo! Hilloo!

THE VALLEY

Hilloo! Hilloo!

(BEELZEBUB *in scraping up the earth turns out a skull.*)

BEELZEBUB

Old one, old one.
Now ere I break you,
Crush you and make you
Clay for my use,
Let me observe you:
You were a bold one
Flat at the dome of you,
Heavy the base of you,
False to the home of you,
Strong was the face of you,
Strange to all fears.
Yet did the hair of you
Hide what you were.
Now to re-nerve you—

(He crushes the skull between his hands and mixes it with the clay.)

Now you are dust,
Limestone and rust.
I mold and I stir
And make you again.

THE VALLEY

Again? Again?

(In the same manner BEELZEBUB *has fashioned several figures, standing them against the trees.)*

LOKI

Now for the breath of life. As I remember
You have done right to mold your creatures first,
And stand them up.

BEELZEBUB

From gravitation
I make the will.

YOGARINDRA

Out of sensation
Comes his ill.
Out of my mirror
Springs his error.
Who was so cruel
To make him the slave
Of me the sorceress, you the knave,
And you the plotter to catch his thought,
Whatever he did, whatever he sought?
With a nature dual
Of will and mind
A thing that sees, and a thing that's blind.
Come! to our dance! Something hated him
Made us over him, therefore fated him.
(*They join hands and dance.*)

LOKI

Passion, reason, custom, rules,
Creeds of the churches, lore of the schools,
Taint in the blood and strength of soul.
Flesh too weak for the will's control;
Poverty, riches, pride of birth,
Wailing, laughter, over the earth,
Here I have you caught again,
Enter my web, ye sons of men.

YOGARINDRA

Look in my mirror! Isn't it real?
What do you think now, what do you feel?
Here is treasure of gold heaped up;
Here is wine in the festal cup.
Tendrils blossoming, turned to whips,
Love with her breasts and scarlet lips.
Breathe in their nostrils.

BEELZEBUB
                              Falsehood's breath,
Out of nothingness into death.
Out of the mold, out of the rocks
Wonder, mockery, paradox!
Soaring spirit, groveling flesh,
Bait the trap, and spread the mesh.
Give him hunger, lure him with truth,
Give him the iris hopes of Youth.
Starve him, shame him, fling him down,
Whirled in the vortex of the town.
Break him, age him, till he curse
The idiot face of the universe.
Over and over we mix the clay,—
What was dust is alive to-day.

THE THREE

Thus is the hell-born tangle wound
Swiftly, swiftly round and round.

BEELZEBUB
        (*Waving his trumpet.*)
You live! Away!

ONE OF THE FIGURES
                        How strange and new!
I am I, and another, too.

ANOTHER FIGURE

I was a sun-dew's leaf, but now
What is this longing?—

ANOTHER FIGURE
                        Earth below
I was a seedling magnet-tipped
Drawn down earth—

ANOTHER FIGURE

            And I was gripped
Electrons in a granite stone,
Now I think.

ANOTHER FIGURE

Oh, how alone!

ANOTHER FIGURE

My lips to thine. Through thee I find
Something alone by love divined!

BEELZEBUB

Begone! No, wait. I have bethought me, friends;
Let's give a play.

(He waves his trumpet.)

To yonder green rooms go.

(The figures disappear.)

YOGARINDRA

Oh, yes, a play! That's very well, I think,
But who will be the audience? I must throw
Illusion over all.

LOKI

            And I must shift
The scenery, and tangle up the plot.

BEELZEBUB

Well, so you shall! Our audience shall come
From yonder graves.

*(He blows his trumpet slightly louder than before. The
scene changes. A stage arises among the graves. The
curtain is down, concealing the creatures just created,*

illuminated halfway up by spectral lights. BEELZEBUB
stands before the curtain.)

BEELZEBUB

(*A terrific blast of the trumpet.*)

Who-o-o-o-o-o!

(*Immediately there is a rustling as of the shells of grass-
hoppers stirred by a wind; and hundreds of the dead,
including those who have appeared in the Anthology,
hurry to the sound of the trumpet.*)

A VOICE

Gabriel! Gabriel!

MANY VOICES

The Judgment day!

BEELZEBUB

             Be quiet, if you please
At least until the stars fall and the moon.

MANY VOICES

Save us! Save us!

(*Beelzebub extends his hands over the audience with a
benedictory motion and restores order.*)

BEELZEBUB

Ladies and gentlemen, your kind attention
To my interpretation of the scene.
I rise to give your fancy comprehension,
And analyze the parts of the machine.
My mood is such that I would not deceive you,
Though still a liar and the father of it,
From judgment's frailty I would retrieve you,

Though falsehood is my art and though I love it.
Down in the habitations whence I rise,
The roots of human sorrow boundless spread.
Long have I watched them draw the strength that
     lies
In clay made richer by the rotting dead.
Here is a blossom, here a twisted stalk,
Here fruit that sourly withers ere its prime;
And here a growth that sprawls across the walk,
Food for the green worm, which it turns to slime.
The ruddy apple with a core of cork
Springs from a root which in a hollow dangles,
Not skillful husbandry nor laborious work
Can save the tree which lightning breaks and tangles.
Why does the bright nasturtium scarcely flower
But that those insects multiply and grow,
Which make it food, and in the very hour
In which the veined leafs and blossoms blow?
Why does a goodly tree, while fast maturing,
Turn crooked branches covered o'er with scale?
Why does the tree whose youth was not assuring
Prosper and bear while all its fellows fail?
I under earth see much. I know the soil.
I know where mold is heavy and where thin.
I see the stones that thwart the ploughman's toil,
The crooked roots of what the priests call sin.
I know all secrets, even to the core,
What seedlings will be upas, pine or laurel;
It cannot change howe'er the field's worked o'er.
Man's what he is and that's the devil's moral.
So with the souls of the ensuing drama
They sprang from certain seed in certain earth.
Behold them in the devil's cyclorama,
Shown in their proper light for all they're worth.
Now to my task: I'll give an exhibition
Of mixing the ingredients of spirit.

(*He waves his wand.*)

Come, crucible, perform your magic mission,
Come, recreative fire, and hover near it!
I'll make a soul, or show how one is made.

(*He waves his wand again. Parti-colored flames appear.*)

This is the woman you shall see anon!

(*A red flame appears.*)

This hectic flame makes all the world afraid:
It was a soldier's scourge which ate the bone.
His daughter bore the lady of the action,
And died at thirty-nine of scrofula.
She was a creature of a sweet attraction,
Whose sex-obsession no one ever saw.

(*A purple flame appears.*)

Lo! this denotes aristocratic strains
Back in the centuries of France's glory.

(*A blue flame appears.*)

And this the will that pulls against the chains
Her father strove until his hair was hoary.
Sorrow and failure made his nature cold,
He never loved the child whose woe is shown,
And hence her passion for the things which gold
Brings in this world of pride, and brings alone.
The human heart that's famished from its birth
Turns to the grosser treasures, that is plain.
Thus aspiration fallen fills the earth
With jungle growths of bitterness and pain.
Of Celtic, Gallic fire our heroine!
Courageous, cruel, passionate and proud.
False, vengeful, cunning, without fear o' sin.
A head that oft is bloody, but not bowed.

Now if she meet a man—suppose our hero,
With whom her chemistry shall war yet mix,
As if she were her Borgia to his Nero,
'Twill look like one of Satan's little tricks!
However, it must be. The world's great garden
Is not all mine. I only sow the tares.
Wheat should be made immune, or else the Warden
Should stop their coming in the world's affairs.
But to our hero! Long ere he was born
I knew what would repel him and attract.
Such spirit mathematics, fig or thorn,
I can prognosticate before the fact.

(*A yellow flame appears.*)

This is a grandsire's treason in an orchard
Against a maid whose nature with his mated.

(*Lurid flames appear.*)

And this his memory distrait and tortured,
Which marked the child with hate because she
    hated.
Our heroine's grand dame was that maid's own
    cousin—
But never this our man and woman knew.
The child, in time, of lovers had a dozen,
Then wed a gentleman upright and true.
And thus our hero had a double nature:
One half of him was bad, the other good.
The devil must exhaust his nomenclature
To make this puzzle rightly understood.
But when our hero and our heroine met
They were at once attracted, the repulsion
Was hidden under Passion, with her net
Which must enmesh you ere you feel revulsion.
The virus coursing in the soldier's blood,
The orchard's ghost, the unknown kinship 'twixt

them,
Our hero's mother's lovers round them stood,
Shadows that smiled to see how Fate had fixed
　　them.
This twain pledge vows and marry, that's the play.
And then the tragic features rise and deepen.
He is a tender husband. When away
The serpents from the orchard slyly creep in.
Our heroine, born of spirit none too loyal,
Picks fruit of knowledge—leaves the tree of life.
Her fancy turns to France corrupt and royal,
Soon she forgets her duty as a wife.
You know the rest, so far as that's concerned,
She met exposure and her husband slew her.
He lost his reason, for the love she spurned.
He prized her as his own—how slight he knew her.

(*He waves a wand, showing a man in a prison cell.*)

Now here he sits condemned to mount the gallows—
He could not tell his story—he is dumb.
Love, says your poets, is a grace that hallows,
I call it suffering and martyrdom.
The judge with pointed finger says, "You killed
　　her."
Well, so he did—but here's the explanation;
He could not give it. I, the drama-builder,
Show you the various truths and their relation.

(*He waves his wand.*)

Now, to begin. The curtain is ascending,
They meet at tea upon a flowery lawn.
Fair, is it not? How sweet their souls are blending—
The author calls the play "Laocoon."

A VOICE
Only an earth dream.

ANOTHER VOICE

With which we are done.
A flash of a comet
Upon the earth stream.

ANOTHER VOICE

A dream twice removed,
A spectral confusion
Of earth's dread illusion.

A FAR VOICE

These are the ghosts
From the desolate coasts.
Would you go to them?
Only pursue them.
Whatever enshrined is
Within you is you.
In a place where no wind is,
Out of the damps,
Be ye as lamps.
Flame-like aspire,
To me alone true,
The Life and the Fire.

(BEELZEBUB, LOKI *and* YOGARINDRA *vanish. The phantas-*
magoria fades out. Where the dead seemed to have as-
sembled, only heaps of leaves appear. There is the light
as of dawn. Voices of Spring.)

FIRST VOICE

The springtime is come, the winter departed,
She wakens from slumber and dances light-hearted.
The sun is returning
We are done with alarms,
Earth lifts her face burning,
Held close in his arms.
The sun is an eagle
Who broods o'er his young,

The earth is his nursling
In whom he has flung
The life-flame in seed,
In blossom desire,
Till fire become life,
And life become fire.

SECOND VOICE
I slip and I vanish,
I baffle your eye;
I dive and I climb,
I change and I fly.
You have me, you lose me,
Who have me too well,
Now find me and use me—
I am here in a cell.

THIRD VOICE
You are there in a cell?
Oh, now for a rod
With which to divine you—

SECOND VOICE
Nay, child, I am God.

FOURTH VOICE
When the waking waters rise from their beds of
    snow, under the hill,
In little rooms of stone where they sleep when ici-
    cles reign,
The April breezes scurry through woodlands, say-
    ing "Fulfill!
Awaken roots under cover of soil—it is Spring
    again."

Then the sun exults, the moon is at peace, and voices
Call to the silver shadows to lift the flowers from
    their dreams.

And a longing, longing enters my heart of sorrow,
    my heart that rejoices
In the fleeting glimpse of a shining face, and her hair
    that gleams.

I arise and follow alone for hours the winding way
    by the river,
Hunting a vanishing light, and a solace for joy too
    deep.
Where do you lead me, wild one, on and on forever?
Over the hill, over the hill, and down to the meadows
    of sleep.

THE SUN

Over the soundless depths of space for a hundred
    million miles
Speeds the soul of me, silent thunder, struck from a
    harp of fire.
Before my eyes the planets wheel and a universe
    defiles,
I but a luminant speck of dust upborne in a vast
    desire.

What is my universe that obeys me—myself com-
    pelled to obey
A power that holds me and whirls me over a path
    that has no end?
And there are my children who call me great, the
    giver of life and day,
Myself a child who cry for life and know not whither
    I tend.

A million million suns above me, as if the curtain
    of night
Were hung before creation's flame, that shone
    through the weave of the cloth,
Each with its worlds and worlds and worlds crying
    upward for light,

For each is drawn in its course to what?—as the candle draws the moth.

THE MILKY WAY
Orbits unending,
Life never ending,
Power without end.

A VOICE
Wouldst thou be lord,
Not peace but a sword.
Not heart's desire—
Ever aspire.
Worship thy power,
Conquer thy hour,
Sleep not but strive,
So shalt thou live.

INFINITE DEPTHS
Infinite Law,
Infinite Life.

Afterword

One of the most popular books in all of American literature was written by a part-time author who never before or after was as successful. A lawyer by profession, Edgar Lee Masters read widely and wrote voluminously on the side, hiding poetry behind law books and creating manuscripts alongside legal documents. Reading everything he could find prompted Masters to try his hand first at poems and plays and later essays, novels, and biographies. Born in Kansas in 1869, Masters lived the first fifty years of his life in Illinois, first in Spoon River country in Western Illinois and then in Chicago. Not until 1920 did he give up his law practice to become a full-time writer. He then moved to New York and over the next thirty years continued to write works in almost every literary genre. Though he wrote more than fifty books and planned even more, the one work that made him famous happened almost serendipitously.

Spoon River Anthology emerged piecemeal, at first in serialized form and then as a book derived from the passionate hobby of a full-time lawyer and amateur of letters. While arguing one case before the Illinois Supreme Court and another representing a waitresses' union, Masters worked on *Spoon River Anthology* "at odd times," jotting down ideas and poems "on backs of envelopes, margins of newspapers, when I was on the street car, or in court, or at a luncheon, or at night after I had gone to bed." Thus, in what amounted to his spare time, Masters discovered a voice that spoke to and for a public that made the work popular because it expressed what they felt and believed but could not express for themselves.

Both as a lawyer and a writer, Masters was proud to be a "combatant." He was first and foremost a populist who saw great hope for the democratic experiment if matters were left to people rather than being squashed by the rich and powerful with their misuse of institutions. He devoted eight years of his law practice to what would now be called pro bono work for those in need. He was never particularly fond of America's literary establishment, which he felt departed from Whitman's democratic vision only to be hijacked by a privileged intellectual class that preferred narrow specialization in trivialities to the justifiable roar of the visionary. As he wrote in his biography of Whitman, the process is brutal and relentless. "Legalized privileges and partial laws" bring money to the powerful, who then "make the culture of the country" through a pervasive materialism that renders thinkers "cramped and in want." Poets and visionaries who live and work outside that privileged group are "struck down or rendered dumb or bitter." Resistance, Masters notes, is "outlawed in America." With free speech stifled, the only hope for resistance is to "steal through the interplexus of things forbidden" by picking words that "deceive the swine or which are regarded by them as mere poetry and of no dangerous moment." In *Spoon River Anthology* those outlawed and forbidden steal through.

The characters in this book speak from the grave with the wisdom of hindsight and with no risk of retaliation. Few of their speeches are cordial or docile or even pleasant. More often than not, they challenge established opinions, reveal long-harbored resentments, expose hypocrisy, confess to crimes, and display moods ranging from indignation to jealousy to self-pity. We meet angry and bitter individuals, people repressed by the community that shaped them, thinkers who reached insights about what was happening to them too late to do anything about it. We get to know solitary figures whose visions have been trampled, whose ideals gave way to intense unfulfilled longings, whose wit is sardonic or even morose. Why have several generations of readers enjoyed listening to what might be considered unpleasant or even masochistic? Why are we drawn to figures who can never get it right their whole lives and who are still vitriolic whiners in death? Perhaps the answer to the puzzling popularity of these figures is, quite simply, that they express what we feel and believe. In their graveside confessions, we recall and listen to our own dashed ambitions, the roadblocks thrown in our way, the as yet unfulfilled desires and fragmentary visions that live within us. We see ourselves in these beat-up but still tenacious corpses. In holding out hope that we may still have our say, we support their irreverence, applaud their rants, and even identify with their bombast. In our affinity with these often unlikable speakers, a part of what they would call our "soul" seeps out, takes life, and unites us with their experiences.

The heroes, villains, and unknown quantities of *Spoon River Anthology* are still popular today for all of the usual reasons and more. The voices Masters created are individual, believable, and convincing. They express themselves like people we know today. They continue to resonate with us from their own simpler times because they address problems that are still of great concern to us. Their language is fresh and playful and ever new. They also provide the

timeless drama of looking into and beyond the grave
we must all inevitably face. They have the intricate
nuances of Hollywood fright films—whether the innocent scares of Halloween in *Meet Me in St. Louis*
or the terror of a slasher film. These speakers continue to expose not only the hypocrisy of small-town
life but also the realities of the American dream dis-
torted, deferred, butchered. Reading the poems can
be seen as socially sanctioned voyeurism, the stuff
of urban legends, even a precursor to reality TV or
Entertainment Tonight.

No doubt the format of *Spoon River Anthology* ap-
peals in new ways to our sensibilities conditioned by
the Internet. In it, stories are shared and debated with
the reckless abandon of Internet chat rooms, where
everything is true until it is contradicted and all con-
tributors are judge and jury of their own dominions.
In McLuhanesque fashion, Masters shaped structures
that would be comfortably at home in a world of
e-mail exchanges, list serve flowing of data, search
engines that go nearly everywhere, hypertexts that
make us participants, and new patterns resulting
from the digitalization of video and film. While Masters' expanded epitaphs take their place in a tradition
as old (in English) as Ben Jonson's epigrams, they
also anticipate sound bites, twenty-four-seven news
stations, and cyber collage. McLuhan taught us not
only that the medium is the message and that com-
munications revolutions accompanied first the written form and then the printing press and electronic
culture, but also that old media do not disappear but
thrive in new hybrid forms over time. Masters'
poems continue to appeal to readers conditioned by
new technological structures even as they provide a
good old-fashioned "read."

Spoon River Anthology is particularly well suited
to hybridization in its anticipation of the journalistic
"scoop," the evolution of gossip into an art form,

private voices screaming at us in public forums, public voices emerging from the most private places, and even the positioning of anonymity in ongoing global dialogue. Are TV and Internet instant opinion polls any more spontaneous, passionate, or unreliable as the outcries and debates of Spoon River citizens who are still being interviewed and surveyed and polled even after they have passed on? Can any celebrity interview be more exclusive than the ones snatched from the grave? Can the paparazzi be any more invasive or meddling than the narrator on the hill? Do kiss-and-tell autobiographies or trials of the century really add much to tombstone debates? Today we might "Google" the names on the Spoon River tombstones to trace plot threads or create our own newsweekly "where-are-they-now?" feature. In the end one of the biggest reasons these poems hold up for us is that very little in the way they see the world in 1915 would be out of sync with our teleconferencing or blogging, our annoyance with information overload, or the all too frequent ambiguity or outright confusion that follows accidentally pushing "Reply to All." In fact, these people speaking from "the hill" might just sound to us like members of a wired community where everyone is connected online and yet still alone. We surf through or pause at length, sifting and sorting through the tombstone pronouncements that empower each speaker to be author, editor, publisher, and reviewer—and where everyone gets to have the last word. White-collar crime, hypocritical preachers, fake educators, public officials, and private citizens assaulting or defending democracy itself, the deadly silences of wasted or perverted lives—all are exposed in ways that can seem masochistic. Masters portrayed his heroic people on the hill in the tradition of Juvenal's dark satiric figures, who use the raucous and the irreverent to under-

mine through parody the power of constraining institutions and traditions.

Students of popular culture over the last several
decades have come to see this process of attack as a
coping skill or a strategy of evasion, in which we
confer the status of popularity on works that help us
speak our minds, attack or otherwise mock official
or acceptable truths, and undermine the rules of institutions that limit us. Research on how popularity
comes about and how it endures has moved through
several very different approaches. For a long time
popularity was considered mere opinion or at best
consensus, an agreement not only about what is
worth one's time but also the ways in which individual
traits or cultural differences are expressed, exchanged,
valued or devalued, and regulated. This is usually
seen as a form of populism, a more or less harmoni-
ous interaction of wholesome or at least harmless
tastes, a melting pot of differences, or what John
Fiske sees as "a democratic version of elite human-
ism" that "resituates the cultural life of a nation in
the popular rather than the highbrow" (*Understanding Popular Culture*, 20). In other words, this model
of popularity conferred respectability on what had
previously been relegated to categories like the vulgar (as opposed to real culture), or folk art as opposed to high culture or even the academically
tolerated as opposed to the credentialed. Over the
years *Spoon River Anthology* has moved in and out of
these categories and taken on a life of its own in the
spaces in between—as witnessed by critical assess-
ments ranging from the high praise that America at
last had a poet (Pound) to the more guarded ap-
proval that the poems in the collection were "shred-
ded prose" (Howells).

The second way of accounting for popularity paid
much more attention to how the processes of de-

fending ourselves and fighting back were themselves influences on what we enjoyed and why. Books, movies, and popular music are great sources of pleasure—in this view—because they give us ways of fighting back against dominant socioeconomic classes and elite institutions that exert power over us. According to this model, however, we are seldom capable of knowing our own minds because we are part of a mass public that likes whatever it has been conditioned to like. Because it is seen to be mindless, powerless, and the product of intricate manipulation, popularity in this model retains much of what was considered vulgar throughout history. To this way of thinking, people are told (indirectly, usually) what they will find to be popular, or will decide what is popular based on ignorance driven by the power structure or market forces outside their control. At the time of his death in 1950, Masters' understanding of his one hit book's popularity was necessarily planted firmly in these two models. As a result he would have experienced some satisfaction about the good effects of his work's success, as well as disappointment that genuine populist values were in his time short-lived, trampled, or co-opted until they suffocated in the reassertion of an antithesis between high culture and pop art.

But the tenaciousness and assertiveness of the Spoon River voices enabled them to capture people in ways suggested by a third model espoused by John Fiske. According to an approach that has emerged only in the past thirty years, *Spoon River Anthology* remains so popular today because our reading of the work is for us a genuinely empowering activity. Rather than being the product of an idealized but powerless populism or a degrading and ignorant mass taste, the popularity of the work is earned in an arena of struggle where the mechanisms of cultural control are neither sanctioned nor ignored but identified and then evaded, resisted, or at least addressed.

This third way of understanding popularity uses all the elements of the first two but then goes beyond the helplessness or bitterness, the triviality or transience stereotypically associated with a work considered to be popular. According to this theory, the public—with deliberation and at least a certain level of awareness—likes what it likes because experiencing it is an empowering activity. In this way of thinking, *Spoon River Anthology* invites repeated reading over time and across generations because it still voices struggles that persist, resistance we still hope to mount, evasions and avoidances we achieve in reading and writing, and the vitality we feel when presented with the possibility of change. Precisely because the forces of domination, manipulation, and acquiescence Masters described and captured in his poems are still in place, these works of lasting popularity present—for ordinary readers as well as for the privileged—opportunities for resistance, subversion, and creative visions of our own.

And so the enduring music of these people speaking from "the hill" finds its way nearly a century later to a place of prominence on our bookshelves, on the stages of high school, college, and community theater productions, and in class anthologies, CDs, and cyberspace. Masters' inability to match the success of his one major success surely stems in part from not understanding that the popularity of his anthology came about because of—not in spite of— his being combative, subversive, and resistant. His readers, on the other hand, have long understood that success is measured not only by what one overcomes but perhaps equally by how one copes with and attempts to undermine forces that cannot be fully overcome. With the benefit of our hindsight,

Masters would have echoed (in a slightly different context) his Village Atheist's assessment that popularity is not a gift but an achievement and that "only those who strive mightily/Shall possess it."

How do the characters of Spoon River cope? What do they subvert or undermine? There are many answers in these pages. Hod Putt puts the crimes of capitalism on the table right away by reminding us that we did not invent the abuse of bankruptcy laws in order to get "richer than ever." Mrs. Charles Bliss rages about the cold self-righteousness of "preachers and judges." Then there is Reverend Wiley, busy saving people from themselves as he equates morality with the avoidance of social disgrace no matter what unhappiness is caused to others. John Hancock Otis warns against the assumption that people of wealth are less devoted to liberty than the "man who rises to power/From one suspender." We hear also of Clarence Fawcett, persecuted by a ruthless boss as well as by opportunistic journalists; about Seth Compton, the librarian who fought the censorship perpetrated by those afraid of knowledge; from Richard Bone (a very early new historicist?), who recognized that the tributes he carved on tombstones were outright lies; from Harry Wilmans, swept to war by patriotic fervor and shot through the guts before a flag covered him on the hill; from Dorcas Gustine, who was "not beloved" because she spoke her mind; and of Petit, the poet who comes to the realization that he has been blinded his whole life by "little iambics" as "Homer and Whitman roared in the pines."

Does the continuing popularity of all this venting, whining, and menacingly celebratory shouting empower us to express our frustrations and joys, trials and embattlements? In attempting to evade, subvert, or undermine the constraints imposed upon them, the rebel heroes of Spoon River strive to imagine and discover the soul of their humanity. Penniwit, the artist, tricks Judge Somers out of a pose so that he can get to the spontaneity and genuineness that are "the soul of the person." Tennessee Claflin Shope is "the laughing-stock of the village"—especially with those who displayed what they thought was good sense—because he "asserted the sovereignty" of his own soul. Similarly, William Jones lives in wonder "on the march eternal of endless life." Alfonso Churchill was born with a thirst that caused people to jeer whenever he touted "the greatness of man." And there are so many more examples, such as Isaiah Beethoven, who on his deathbed finds that "the soul of the river had entered my soul,/And the gathered power of my soul was moving/So swiftly it seemed to be at rest."

Not everyone is so serene, of course, and for many, anger gives way to depression and despondency. Archibald Higbie loathes the place of his origins so much he aspires to be reincarnated in another place with "all of Spoon River/Rooted out of my soul." Elizabeth Childers, who lost a baby and her own life in childbirth, denounces the pain of disappointment and the poison of love, declaring, "Death is better than Life." Similarly, James Garber captures the longings of so many when he finds no way to ease "the loneliness of the soul." To all these anguished doubters, Lucinda Matlock responds, "What is this I hear of sorrow and weariness,/Anger, discontent and drooping hopes?" Her retort is famous: "It takes life to love Life."

We no doubt read ourselves into these poems and—in the process—make them an abidingly popular expression of who we are or want to be. Somehow the embattled folks of the mythical Western Illinois prairie community still provide models of venting and evading as we engage in communities of our own, build families and careers, run for public office or the condo-association board, exchange ideas in book clubs, or chat on the Internet. Social and economic conditions as well as political institutions are now very like what Masters derided in his own time. Freedom of speech is again under attack. Individuals are still destroyed by gossip, pressures to conform, and sanctimonious leaders. Even more so today a culture industry fed by multinational corporations and government propaganda dominates not only media but elite institutions of power at every level. Where do we look today for protection against censorship and retaliation that are similar to the way the speakers on "the hill" used death as leverage? As long as we still seek paths of resistance and subversion, *Spoon River Anthology* will continue to influence the way we define ourselves in our reading and writing, in bookstores and libraries, in classrooms and cyberspace. We will thrive on the battles of resistance and the subtle and overt undermining. We will identify with those in Spoon River who speak out loudly. Though not beloved by villagers when she spoke her mind, Dorcas Gustine gets it right for us: "The tongue may be an unruly member—/But silence poisons the soul."

—Ronald Primeau

Selected Bibliography

Barnstone, Willis. "Introduction." *The New Spoon River*. New York: Collier, 1924.

Burgess, Charles E. "Edgar Lee Masters: The Lawyer as Writer," in *Vision of This Land*, eds. John E. Hallwas and Dennis J. Reader. Macomb: Western Illinois University, 1976.

Derleth, August. *Three Literary Men*. New York: Candlelight Press, 1963.

Duffey, Bernard. *The Chicago Renaissance in American Letters: A Critical Study*. East Lansing: Michigan State University Press, 1954.

Earnest, Ernest. "Spoon River Revisited." *Western Humanities Review*, winter, 1967.

Flanagan, John T. *Edgar Lee Masters: The Spoon River Poet and His Critics*. Metuchen, NJ: Scarecrow Press, 1974.

Hartley, Lois Teal. *Spoon River Revisited*. Muncie: Ball State Teachers College, 1963.

Kramer, Dale. *Chicago Renaissance: Literary Life in the Midwest 1900–1930*. New York: Appleton, 1968.

Masters, Edgar Lee. *Across Spoon River* (1936). Urbana and Chicago: University of Illinois Press, 1991.

Masters, Hardin W. *Edgar Lee Masters: A Biographical*

Sketchbook About a Famous American Author. Madison, NJ: Fairleigh Dickinson University Press, 1977.

Masters, Hilary. *Last Stands, Notes From Memory.* New York: McGraw Hill, 1983.

Masters, Marcia Lee. *The Wind Around the Moon.* Georgetown: Dragon's Teeth Press, 1986.

Primeau, Ronald. *Beyond Spoon River: The Legacy of Edgar Lee Masters.* Austin: University of Texas Press, 1981.

Putzel, Max. *The Man in the Mirror: William Marion Reedy and His Magazine.* Columbia: University of Missouri Press, 1963.

Robinson, Frank K., *Edgar Lee Masters: An Exhibition in Commemoration of His Birth.* Austin: Harry Ransom Humanities Research Center, 1970.

Russell, Herbert K., ed. (and Introduction to) *The Enduring River: Edgar Lee Masters' Uncollected Spoon River Poems.* Carbondale: Southern Illinois University Press, 1991.

——. "Edgar Lee Masters' Final Years in the Midwest." *Essays in Literature,* fall, 1977.

——. *Edgar Lee Masters: A Biography.* Urbana and Chicago: University of Illinois Press, 2005.

Untermeyer, Louis. *American Poetry Since 1900.* New York: Henry Holt, 1923.

Wrenn, John H., and Margaret H. Wrenn. *Edgar Lee Masters.* Boston: Twayne 1983.

Yatron, Michael. *America's Literary Revolt.* New York: Philosophical Library, 1959.

AMERICAN VOICES

THE JUNGLE by Upton Sinclair
In writing some of the most harrowing scenes ever in modern literature, Upton Sinclair vividly depicted factory life in Chicago in the first years of the 20th century.

O PIONEERS! by Willa Cather
Alexandra Bergson inherits her father's failing farm, raises her brothers alone, and is torn by the emergence of an unexpected passion.

THE SONG OF THE LARK by Willa Cather
Thea Kronberg is a feisty girl whose upbringing in a raw, provincial Colorado town nearly stifles her artistic ambitions. Here is a wonderful portrait of a young woman who makes her own destiny.

WINESBURG, OHIO by Sherwood Anderson
Combines Sherwood Anderson's memories of his boyhood in Clyde, Ohio, and his observations in turn-of-the-century Chicago. A modern American classic that embraces frankness and truth, it deals with people whose deeply moving lives are filled with secrets.

From the
American Renaissance

BILLY BUDD & Other Tales
Herman Melville
Collected here are Melville's greatest stories, wry and insightful,
tragic and moving—some of the most vivid writing in literature.

TWO YEARS BEFORE THE MAST
Richard Henry Dana, Jr.
One of the most engaging recreations of life at sea ever published. In
1834, Dana signed on as a common seaman for a perilous voyage to
California. This is his record of the joys and hardships of a sailor's life.
The result is both a protest against brutal working conditions and a
powerful portrayal of courage and endurance.

LEAVES OF GRASS
Walt Whitman
Here are the incomparable poems of one of America's greatest
poets—singer, thinker, visionary, and citizen extraordinaire. Henry
David Thoreau said of him, "probably the greatest democrat that ever
lived." This edition is Whitman's final authorized and complete version
of his work.

THE SCARLET LETTER
Nathaniel Hawthorne
Hawthorne's masterpiece is a tale of deceit, adultery, shame, and
redemption. It provides a tremendously moving insight into the passions
of the human heart, and the power of the human psyche.

Read more about the
Early American Experience

THE AUTOBIOGRAPHY & OTHER WRITINGS
    Benjamin Franklin
The Autobiography provides important insights into the mind
of one of the founders of American democracy. This volume
also includes "The Way to Wealth," "Essays to Do Good,"
selections from his scientific and political work, and writings
on family, life, and religion.

THE LAST OF THE MOHICANS
    James Fenimore Cooper
Moving with the speed of a classic western novel, this story
tells of the adventures of Natty Bumppo and Chingachgook
as they travel through hostile territory in Canada and
Upstate New York during the French and Indian War.

THE LEGEND OF SLEEPY HOLLOW
& OTHER STORIES IN THE SKETCH BOOK
    Washington Irving
Sage, storyteller, wit, and keen observer of the American way
of life, Irving has been called, "the first ambassador the new
world of letters has sent to the old."

READ THE TOP 20
SIGNET CLASSICS

PENGUIN.COM
FACEBOOK.COM/SIGNETCLASSIC